THE DARK ED
INSANITY

Ann Preston shivered and lit a cigarette, aware that her fingers were shaking. Certainly her introduction to the house of Duval had not gone as expected. But Pierre, the man she had been warned against, was certainly not the person to be feared; if he was insane, it was a strange form of insanity indeed.

Rather, the chateau itself seemed to be the breeding ground of evil. The ghost of Gaston Duval, the strange scent of lilies of the valley, Marie's frightened eyes as she warned Ann not to stay in the house . . . these were not calculated to make her feel at ease. She told herself that she was behaving like a frightened schoolgirl. What possible harm could come to her? She was safe in her room, the door locked against intruders . . . and then she froze, mouth open, eyes wide.

Someone was outside the room—turning the door handle!

**PUT PLEASURE IN YOUR READING
Larger type makes the difference**
This EASY EYE Edition is set in large, clear type—at least 30 percent larger than usual. It is printed on scientifically tinted non-glare paper for better contrast and less eyestrain.

STRANGER IN A DARK LAND
Julie Wellsley

PRESTIGE BOOKS • NEW YORK

STRANGER IN A DARK LAND

Copyright © 1969 by Press Editorial Services, Ltd.
All rights reserved
Printed in the U.S.A.

PRESTIGE BOOKS INC. • 18 EAST 41ST STREET
NEW YORK, N.Y. 10017

Chapter One

With the sun glinting on its fuselage, the jet came out of the cloudless blue sky and Ann Preston felt once more that old familiar quickening of her pulse as the plane touched down on French soil. She supposed it was because she had spent her childhood in the tiny but picturesque village in the south of France and had always looked upon France as her mother country.

For one thing, everyone had been so kind there after her father had died in that terrible air disaster in Brazil. She had been a little girl then with wide brown eyes and blonde pigtails—a pretty child, dazed and bewildered and heartbroken, for she had worshiped the big, cheery man with the battered felt hat who used to hoist her up onto his shoulders and carry her up to the house.

He had been a happy man with a booming voice and laughter in his eyes. A giant of a man who came striding down the garden path, his arms full of mysterious packages of all shapes and sizes for her. He never forgot; it was always the same whenever he came home from a trip. For years he had been father and mother to her, for her mother had died when she was born.

What he did and how he made his money she never knew until she was much older. An explorer, her Aunt Peggy said one day in answer to her question, and lying in her darkened attic room at night, she would conjure up pictures of him fighting lions and tigers, battling with alligators in steamy jungle swamps.

He, too, had loved France. He had loved to see the dew sparkling on freshly cut blooms in the flower market at dawn, the village square at holiday time with its garishly painted roundabouts and blaring organs, the hot doughnut stalls, the colorful cafés and *estaminets,* the vineyards, the stately majestic chateaux, the silent green forests and the golden beaches.

He had loved the people in all their moods, happy and sad. He would silently watch the laughing shapely girls with their provocative eyes; he would yarn for hours with the men of the soil in their blue berets as they sat and drank the local wine in a smoke-filled bistro.

And, sometimes, she would hear him sob in his sleep and she would wonder why—

She came to reality with a start, suddenly conscious of a pair of dark, quizzical eyes appraising her from a lean bronzed face creased by a smile—an attractive smile that crinkled the corners of his mouth, made little lights glint in the depths of his eyes.

"Your first visit to France?"

She liked his voice, it was a low, rather pleasant drawl, and he had nice white teeth. She shook her head. She wasn't in the habit of being picked up in airport lounges in southern France like this, but she remembered seeing him board the plane at London airport and had been attracted by his lean good looks. There was something very nice about him, and the after-shave he used reminded her of her father. She found herself responding to his infectious grin.

"No, I've been here before."

"Just my luck."

Tall, with thick, very black, unruly hair he looked thirtyish, but was probably younger. He wore a beautifully tailored dark blue suit, a cream silk shirt, and a blue tie. He carried a brown leather briefcase, and there was a neatly folded newspaper under his arm.

"Then obviously you know your way around," he said. "Everything's against me."

Her eyes twinkled. "For what?"

"A kidnaping."

"I'm sorry if I've spoiled your plans."

"I had it all figured out. I would strike up an acquaintance on the plane, and afterwards everything would be smooth sailing."

"What went wrong?"

"The man with the beard and thick black-rimmed specs prevented the crime. He is probably a secret agent in disguise."

Odd he should say that. There had been something about the portly little man sitting across from her wearing a beard and black sunglasses that had made her feel distinctly uneasy, but she couldn't exactly put her finger on what it was that repelled her.

It could have been his eyes. Once, when he had removed the glasses, she had realized that his eyes were glassy and protuberant; their unblinking gaze had sent shivers down her spine. Yet his manner had been pleasant enough, although he was inclined to laugh and smile too much. She had always been a little wary of such men, suspecting that they had a darker side to their natures that they were anxious to conceal from the world.

"You're not listening!" came the stranger's accusing voice.

"I'm sorry. Do forgive me." Her eyes teased him. "I was wondering how you would have kidnapped me!"

He had picked up her case as though they were travelling together.

"A very large, very luxurious car would have whispered alongside. My chauffeur always meets me; I would have explained. I would have insisted upon escorting you to your hotel, but instead you would have been spirited away to my hideout in the Pyrenees. You'd have been my prisoner until your parents paid the ransom money in full."

"They're both dead," she said quietly.

"I'm sorry." He spoke quickly, the bantering tone gone. He should have guessed, he thought. There was a sadness in her soft brown eyes that time had been unable to erase. He had wondered about it at London airport. There had been a wistfulness about her: a little-girl-lost expression on a heart-shaped face. He had intended to approach her when he had been forestalled by an elderly traveler with a lecherous eye.

She was undoubtedly the prettiest girl on the flight: petite but with large eyes, a warm full mouth and silky blonde hair cascading down past her shoulders. She wore a pale pink mini-dress with a V neckline, and when she smiled her cheeks dimpled attractively. Everything she wore, even her shoes, were new but not expensive . . . a secretary, he had thought, probably on vacation. The kind of girl you dream about, only to wake and find yourself staring into the lack-luster eyes of your landlady who, although she was a sweetie, never looked her best with colored curlers in her hair, a cigarette stub smouldering between her lips, and a morning cup of lukewarm tea in her hand.

They had crossed the half-empty lounge and reached the double glass doors. "Thank you for carrying my case. I can get a cab here." It looked, Ann thought, as though Aunt Peggy had been unable to meet her. But her companion was shaking his head.

"Probably be driven by a white-slaver," he said solemnly. "I refuse to leave you until I know you're perfectly safe. And I suggest a drink first."

She hesitated, then nodded. Why not? She had all the time in the world. "If you promise not to kidnap me afterwards!"

"That's a deal. At least, not until you decide to return to London."

"I'm afraid that won't be for a while."

They sat up at the quilted, curved bar on green leather and chromium stools. The white-coated barman with sleek, well-groomed hair was attentive. Her companion ordered a cognac for himself, a *vin blanc avec citron* for Ann.

"It's good to be home," she murmured.

"You live here?"

"I did as a child—with a distant relative on my father's side. She has a small cottage at Gazon."

"Why that's great! I've booked a room at the

Continentale. Perhaps we could see each other again?"

"That would be nice."

"You'll be staying with your relatives?"

"Yes. I thought Tom would meet me but he obviously couldn't make it."

He offered cigarettes from a crumpled packet. "Tom?"

"My cousin. Aunt Peggy's son."

"Oh." He was silent for a moment, thoughtful. He hadn't missed the sudden sparkle that had come to her eyes. She was in love with the man, he supposed; perhaps they intended to marry. . . . "Here we are, talking like old friends. We'll be seeing each other in the village, and I don't even know your name!"

"Ann—Ann Preston, Mr. Martin."

He looked surprised. "You know my name?"

"You'll never guess how."

"You're a mind reader."

She laughed. "It's on the label attached to your briefcase."

He made a face. "I'm not very bright, am I? The S is for Steve."

"You're here on business?"

"I'm here to do research for a book I've been commissioned to write on French chateaux."

"You're a writer?"

"Of sorts," he acknowledged.

"Have you had any books published?"

"No," he said after a moment's pause. "This will be my first. Until now I've specialized in short stories—but that's enough about me." He said it quickly, as though not anxious to talk about himself. "Are you here on vacation?"

"No, I'm working too." She stubbed out her cigarette. "I had a dull and dreary job with a firm of exporters in London, and quite by chance I met this man who told me there was a good job going with the Duval family; they wanted a secretary, and the money was particularly good. I jumped at it because I needed a change, and because I would be able to live with Peggy—" She broke off, for his eyes had narrowed.

"Not—Pierre Duval?" he said.

"Why, yes. Do you know him?"

"Only by name," he said hurriedly. "I came across it in a reference book. As a matter of fact, the Duval chateau is one of those I am hoping to visit."

"Then I'll do what I can to arrange it for you."

"That's very kind of you. If you've lived in these parts you know the Duval family, then?"

"Only of them," she said.

"I see." He massaged his chin slowly. "According to the reference book the chateau is supposed to be haunted."

"That's news to me. But of course, I was very young at the time, and such things wouldn't have been discussed in front of a small girl with large ears." She smiled.

"They're very pretty ears," he grinned back. "Apparently it's a comparatively new ghost—the son of the house."

Her forehead furrowed. "I suppose that would be Gaston Duval."

"That's the name! He was with the French forces in Dien Bien Phu, an espionage agent who was captured and horribly tortured. He finally succeeded in escaping and making his way back to the French forces, but he was a broken man and died soon afterwards." He paused. "His ghost was seen soon afterwards, they say."

Ann shivered. "Don't tell me any more or I shall begin to wish I hadn't taken the job!"

It was to become her most fervent wish, and not in the very distant future, either.

The man with the black-rimmed sunglasses waddled past the bar doors, thumbing tobacco into a battered pipe. His shoulders were hunched as though the driving coat he wore was too heavy for him. On his head, at a jaunty angle, was a gray linen hat he had bought in Biarritz a week earlier.

From Biarritz, Vorrelli had flown to Washington to attend a conference of hard-eyed, cigar-smoking men seated around a long table in a walnut-panelled board room, on the twenty-second floor of a glass and concrete skyscraper. He had stayed an hour, then flown to Britain, before returning to France.

A sleek black car with two men sitting in it was parked outside a newly painted cafe with blue shutters where one could sit all day beneath a red and white umbrella, enjoy black coffee and cognac, and watch the world go by—or perhaps in the idiom of the man standing on the corner, the girls.

Max lit a cigarette and flicked the spent match toward an empty cup standing on one of the tables. He winked when it disappeared into the cup.

"Jackpot," he crooned and sucked noisily on the cigarette. "Any luck?" He leaned out of the car window, squinting through the blue tobacco smoke that spiraled upwards from the cigarette held loosely between his blubbery lips.

"Yes, Max," Vorrelli answered.

"Good." A few moments passed, and then Max broke into a paroxysm of violent coughing, his thin pallid face contorted. "Bloody French weeds," he choked. His face was purple, his eyes watery.

Vorrelli smiled thinly. "They'll be the death of you, Max. Take my advice: give them up."

"I'd sooner die."

"You'd miss the chicks."

"Yeah!" Max brightened visibly. "Which reminds me, you shoulda seen this French piece just now, her skirt was right up to—"

"Spare me the details." The man behind the sunglasses sighed. He removed them carefully, wiped them with a red silk scarf, and replaced them on his beaklike nose. There were times, he reflected, when he wondered if Max was worth the money he paid him. There was only one subject on his mind, and after a while he became annoying. But Max had worked with him a long time: Vorrelli could read his mind, knew his reactions to most situations. Max was no danger to Vorrelli. He said, "I've been checking."

"And?"

"This is the place."

"Where do we stay?" Max queried.

"I saw a rental agent in Biarritz. There's a small villa about two miles from the chateau. We stay there."

"Who's going to look after us?" Max grumbled. "We gotta eat."

"A young French girl."

"Yeah?" The hooded eyes flickered interest. "Live in?"

"No!"

"Oh." He looked disappointed.

"And, Max?"

"Yeah?"

"No funny business. We don't want any talk in the village."

"Okay if you say so, but—"

"I do say so," Vorrelli stated finally.

Max stared glumly through the window, and whistled tonelessly through his teeth.

"How was Washington?"

"Fine," Vorrelli said. "The girl's name is Ann —Ann Preston. I came over on the same flight with her."

"Where is she now?"

"In the airport bar. She's with a guy she met." He frowned and stoked his beard. "Familiar, too. It's had me puzzled. I've seen him around somewhere . . . it'll come to me; it always does."

"Maybe I'll remember him," Max said.

"Since when did you remember anything?" Vorrelli said irritably.

Max said sourly, "I might." He lit another cigarette and wheezed. "What's her name?"

"I've already told you. Ann, you fool!"

"Ann Yu Ful? That's a screwy name, ain't it? She a Chink?"

Oh God, whispered Vorrelli. I can see it's going to be one of those days! Then he stiffened. "That's her."

Ann had emerged from the bar with Steve Martin. They were talking animatedly.

Max gave a soft whistle. "I didn't think they made them like that any more!"

"She's the one we want. Just remember her."

"As if I could forget," protested Max. "I thought you said she was a Chink?"

Chapter Two

Peggy Langognes was a tall, elegant woman who looked what she was: smart, sophisticated, ageless. She had very black hair, brushed till it gleamed, and tied at the nape of her neck with a small black bow. She wore a blue silk mandarin shirt and orange slacks when she came down the white-painted staircase with her arms outstretched.

"Ann! It is wonderful to see you again!"

"Peggy! Oh, it's good to be home!"

Peggy embraced her affectionately. "Forgive me for not meeting you, but I've been terribly busy with Tom not well, poor dear."

"Of course I forgive you. But I'm sorry about Tom. Is he better?"

"Oh yes—it was just a touch of flu. But let me look at you, darling." She held Ann at arm's length. "You were a pretty thing as a child, but now you're a vision!"

"Nonsense!" Ann laughed. She felt wonderfully happy now that she was with Peggy again. It was almost five years since they had met, and her aunt hadn't changed in any way, as far as Ann could see: still as sweet; just as elegant.

Peggy finally released her, and there was a hint of tears in her eyes.

"Darling, how proud your father would be . . . but we'll talk later. I'll show you to your room. I'm sure you want to clean up. It's your old room, dear—I know you always liked it."

Ann felt she was really home when she climbed the flight of winding stairs and reached the attic. It was still snug and so cozy with its sloping roof. The divan with its gay chintz cover stood beneath the window, and she knelt on it to gaze out over the green fields toward the distant hills . . . nothing had changed. She said softly, "So peaceful. I've thought of it often."

"I can guess. Tom insisted on changing rooms when I told him how much it meant to you." She gazed at Ann with affection. How lovely she had grown; what a picture!

"Oh!" Ann exclaimed. "Any other room would have done just as well. Tom shouldn't—"

"I tell you, he didn't mind in the least."

"It does seem so unfair."

"Rubbish!" came a voice from the doorway.

Tom was only twenty-four but already he had quite a reputation as a scientist. He had grown from a pink-faced, bright-eyed schoolboy with inky fingers into a broad-shouldered young man with a fair, clipped moustache. He reminded Ann of a prosperous farmer with his brown tweed hacking jacket and creased gray flannels, and she blinked. How he had changed!

"Tom! I wouldn't have known you." She suddenly felt just a little shy. "It was sweet of you to change rooms."

"Forget it," he said gruffly.

He seemed a little shy himself, almost ill at ease after his first, very intent stare from the doorway, and after enquiring if she had enjoyed the trip, he excused himself, and Ann heard his slow heavy tread descend the stairs.

Peggy stared after him affectionately. "Tom's not much of a talker. He lives and sleeps science, and he has a lot on his mind at present. Some new project, I believe. Now give me a couple of minutes and I'll brew a pot of tea."

For the next hour or two they exchanged news in the gray-stoned living room with its bright curtaining, and then the conversation veered around to Ann's new job.

"I can't say I'm too happy about your working at the chateau," Peggy murmured, lighting a menthol cigarette and studying Ann thoughtfully.

"Good heavens, why not?"

The older woman shrugged. "For one thing, it's

a gloomy, depressing place in a lonely desolate spot, and I think it would get on your nerves. I've been there, and quite frankly I was glad when it was behind me. I'd called to see one of the maids who worked there. The place has an *atmosphere* —I don't know how to explain it. For one thing, it's as silent as a tomb. It's dark and brooding, as though . . . oh, I don't know . . . As though the house had life, as though it were possessed by something evil and malignant."

"The locals avoid it like the plague," Tom said, leaning forward. He hadn't taken his eyes off Ann from the moment she had arrived.

Ann smiled faintly. "Probably because it's alleged to be haunted."

"So—how you know about that, Ann?"

"Someone on the plane told me about it, but I've never believed in ghosts. It's a lot of nonsense. But you know how superstitious some country people are. I mean, some believe that if a bee flies into a house it's a messenger of death!"

"That's not so peculiar as you think," Peggy observed quietly. "I've known it to happen on two or three occasions."

"Next you'll be telling me that you believe a howling dog is a similar bad omen!"

"And I've known that to come true." Tom grunted. "There are even stranger things—"

"Well, I'm not superstitious, and never have

been," Ann cut in crisply. "Anyway, I shall be glad of some peace and quiet after 'swinging London.' Let's face it, I'm a country girl at heart, and noise, crowds, traffic jams are not for me. I've had enough of it."

"You'll change your mind after a few weeks at the chateau."

Ann lit another cigarette. "We'll just have to see . . . but I shall be returning here every evening; I will be no different from any other working girl living at home." She hesitated. "I don't think you quite realize what it's like living in the city. It's a very lonely existence. You know so few people, and you can't afford to go out every night. After a while you begin to think you're in prison. Just the daily routine and nothing to do in the evenings, once you've done your chores, except read or listen to the radio—or just sit! Sometimes you could scream."

"Well, now you're here I must make up for all that," said Tom, patting her hand.

There was something about the way that he looked at her that made her bite her lip. From the glances that he had given her, the way he seized every opportunity to touch her, it was plain that Tom found her more than attractive—and that could make for complications and embarrassment.

It wasn't that she didn't like him. She did and always had. But now they were grown up. He was a man and she was a woman. He was not the kind of man she would want to marry. If she ever did, she thought, it would be to someone rather like Steve Martin, a dark man, good looking, with smiling eyes and a sense of humor.

She lowered her gaze, coloring beneath his frankly admiring stare.

"Tell me something about the Duvals," she said hurriedly.

"No one really knows much about them," Peggy said. "The family has always kept very much to itself. They've been here for generations and are considered to be wealthy, but there's been a rumor of late that their fortunes have changed. Whether or not this is true, I don't know."

"Tell me something about the members of the family. I only met their agent in London."

"There are three in the family." Tom patted his jacket pocket, seeking his tobacco pouch. "There *were* four."

"Oh yes, I heard about Gaston. Isn't there a daughter, Yvette? What is she like?"

"Very beautiful—hard brittle loveliness, however. She seems keyed up and highly strung."

Peggy looked surprised. "I didn't know you knew her, Tom."

"I met her once," he said casually. "It was in Paris. Didn't I tell you? She was modeling for an artist in Montmartre. I can't say I really took to her.

She struck me as being the callous grasping type, and if she wanted anything, nothing would stop her from getting it." He looked absently through the window. "She had a string of men friends, and she could and would twist them all around her little finger."

"Does she have anything to do with the running of the estate?"

"No, I doubt it. I had the impression she wasn't so much interested in the making of money as in the spending of it."

Peggy said, "I should imagine Pierre Duval looks after the Duval estates, and I suspect they are many. No one ever sees him; he is something of a recluse. He's supposed to have widely traveled in his youth."

"And Madame Duval?"

"Like her husband, she does not go far, but I am told she still mourns the death of her son. Some say that she will never recover from the shock, and that his room has not been touched since the night he died . . . so you can imagine why I'm not happy at the thought of a young and cheerful girl like yourself working in such an atmosphere."

Rising to his feet, Tom said, "It's your first night in France after so long, Ann. Let's go out and celebrate. We'll drive into Biarritz. Coming, mother?"

"No, dear, I've too much to do."

"But we can't leave you alone!" protested Ann.

"Of course you can." Peggy was already putting the teacups on the tray. "I've an idea floating about in my head, and I want to have a quiet cup of coffee and think about it."

"Well, if you're sure you don't mind . . ."

"Of course I don't, darling. You're only young once. Go out and enjoy yourselves."

"Then I'll go up and change, Tom."

Peggy watched her as she made her way upstairs. She wasn't, she mused, the striking beauty her mother was, but she had the same olive-tinted skin, large expressive eyes, and generous mouth.

She found it difficult to believe that this attractive young woman was the child who had once modeled her own dress creations when Peggy, for want of something to occupy her mind, had tried her hand at designing children's dresses—and had become an immediate success. Sometimes, looking back, she thought she owed much of that success to her pretty child model's large-eyed simplicity.

Meanwhile Ann had changed into a simple powder blue dress. She wondered, with a sudden quickening of her heart, if they would encounter Steve Martin while they were in town, and then quickly told herself that it wasn't fair to Tom, who was so obviously looking forward to spending an evening with her.

"You look wonderful, Ann," he breathed when she came downstairs. "Doesn't she, mother?"

"Fabulous, darling, as they say these days." She kissed Ann lightly on the cheek. "Now, off with you and enjoy yourselves."

It did not take them long to reach town in Tom's battered Citroen. They slid to a stop in a small tree-lined square just outside the flower market. There were rotting fruits and vegetables in the gutter. Earlier, Tom explained, the square had been filled with wooden stalls. The small farmers from the outlying districts had brought in fresh vegetables; stall owners had shouted their wares to the jostling crowds. Ann could imagine the scene, rather like Petticoat Lane on a Sunday morning.

The club to which Tom escorted her was in a narrow alley just off the square. The entrance was neon lit, and the richly carpeted foyer was faintly perfumed. Glass doors led to an American bar and the club room. Inside it was small and intimate, with its orange-quilted walls and discreet lighting.

The tables surrounding the dance floor were covered with crisply starched linen and glittering cutlery. Plump, tuxedo-clad businessmen puffed fat cigars or held tightly sheathed girls close as they danced to soft, haunting music. The air was heavy with exotic perfumes and fragrant tobacco. Obsequious waiters padded between the tables where guests talked, laughed, gesticulated as champagne corks popped. It was a long way from a studio apartment with a hot plate and a cracked ceiling in Stamford Hill.

"Like it, Ann?"

"Very much."

They were shown to a table near the floor. Tom ordered two martinis and an excellent meal, and then led her onto the floor.

"It's really wonderful to see you again," he said softly. His arm tightened about her waist. "I was feeling pretty low until you arrived; things haven't been going too well for me lately."

"Oh, what do you mean?"

"I've had shocking bouts of depression, been taking long walks at night because I couldn't sleep. But now it's going to be all right, I know it is."

"If you're not sleeping, Tom, you should see a doctor."

Tom grimaced. "That fool! He's never sober. But don't worry, I'll be okay."

She gazed up at him. "Is something worrying you, Tom?"

"No, of course not, just the usual business worries, nothing more. Times are changing, one has to keep up with the modern trend . . . but don't let's be so serious! We're here to enjoy ourselves."

It was toward the end of the evening when they were leaving that she saw Steve Martin. He was standing at the end of the bar, a glass raised to his lips in a toast. Smiling up at him was a beautiful, teenage girl in a scarlet evening gown that clung lovingly to her shapely figure. She had long, straight black hair that flowed way down past her creamy shoulders and dark slightly almond-shaped eyes. Her mouth was sensual, vividly painted. Diamond clips sparkled at her ears.

"Yvette Duval," murmured Tom, as he steered Ann toward the entrance. "Can't say I've seen the chap before."

"His name is Steve Martin," Ann said and felt strange.

"You know him?" He looked surprised.

"We met coming over."

"He's on vacation?"

"No. He's a writer, here to do research for a new book."

"I see."

He looked thoughtful as he drove home along the wide, tree-lined road, speeding past small stone cottages and vineyards. He didn't slacken speed as they drove through dark, silent villages with closed shutters and probing church spires, and at last he swung up the short drive to the garage beside Peggy's large cottage.

"I hope you've enjoyed your first evening, Ann," he said softly when the car stopped.

"I have—very much."

"Good. We will do it again."

She thought for a moment he was going to kiss her, but he seemed suddenly to change his mind. She bit her lip. Tom had always been attractive to her—she had realized that the last time they had met. He had been very shy then, but five years had changed him. He was bolder, more confident, and it worried her. It could prove awkward living under the same roof.

She liked him enormously, but he was not the type of man she would like to marry—especially since she had met Steve Martin.

She felt a faint twinge of jealousy as she thought of the beautiful Yvette who had been with him. It had not crossed her mind that they would know each other . . . but perhaps they had met in Paris. Certainly she was very lovely; the kind of girl, Ann thought, who would be attractive to any man.

"Perhaps we ought to go in now." Tom's voice broke into her thoughts.

He sounded a little sad, so on an impulse she gave him a quick peck on the cheek. "Thanks for a lovely evening, Tom." She swung her legs out of the car.

He started to say something, but changed his mind and followed her up to the cottage door.

The night was dark, and there was no moon; the scent of roses hung on the air. Something rustled in the bushes nearby and, startled, she turned her head sharply. She could almost have sworn she glimpsed the pale blur of a face in the bushes, and then it was gone, and Tom was opening the door and ushering her inside.

It must have been her imagination, she thought. After all, who would want to spy on them?

Chapter Three

Peggy insisted upon driving Ann the fifteen miles to the chateau at La Beffini. Tom had already left in the Citroen, but there had been a good-luck note slipped under her door. It was a kind thought, and she wondered if in similar circumstances Steve would have done the same. Probably, she decided, with roses freshly cut from the garden.

"My dear, it's no bother," Peggy had exclaimed when she had protested that she could catch a bus. "Besides, I enjoy a run first thing in the morning to blow the cobwebs away, especially if I've been working the previous night."

"But I could so easily catch the bus—"

"Well, it's not necessary. Either Tom or I will pick you up tonight."

"Perhaps by then he will have found a little runabout for me. Nothing too expensive, of course; all it needs is four wheels and no starting troubles."

"I know, dear, but you may have to wait a day or two."

It was not the best of mornings for starting a new job. The sky was gray and overcast, and it was raining a fine but heavy rain. Water was gurgling down from a drainpipe, and a drain blocked with leaves was overflowing. It grew even darker as they drove, and soon forked lightning split the sky, immediately followed by a vicious clap of thunder.

When at last they came in sight of the Chateau Duval, Ann's heart sank. It was a somber forbidding building of red brick with gray roofed towers at each corner; it reminded her of an old castle she had once seen on the banks of the Rhine. There were creepers breaking away from the old walls, and they whispered gently as the breeze rustled through the dead leaves. The gray, dusty windows were like unseeing eyes.

It must have been hundreds of years old, and now most of it was falling into ruin. There was a gap high up in the crenellated walls where part of it had crumbled away and crashed down. No attempt had been made to remove the rubble heaped at the foot of the wall. The once-beautiful gardens were overgrown with weeds, and the stench of rotting vegetation filled the air. The concrete paths were cracked and moss covered, sprouting tufts of grass. Even the trees and shrubs growing near the edge of the lake were bent and crooked; their gaunt nightmarish shapes resembled tortured spirits who had given up all hope of escape and now, bowed with despair, leaned suicidally toward the scum-covered water.

Ann's eyes came back to the dark, brooding house, and she felt a little shiver. It seemed somehow to emanate evil, a house without a soul, without warmth, without laughter. It must have been a house that had known only tears and heartbreak —a house that had died.

Ann lifted the black knocker in the heavily studded oak door. Long after she had knocked she heard its echo continue through the corridors of the old house.

Then suddenly the door creaked open, almost protestingly, as though the chateau itself resented being awakened.

The man who stood there was tall and thin, with a shock of white hair that flowed back from a lined, weatherbeaten forehead. His features were gaunt, with sunken eyes and yellowed cheeks; his mouth was a thin gash. He wore a faded black jacket and striped trousers, shiny at the knees; he was stoop shouldered and smelt of whiskey.

"M'amselle?"

"I am Ann Preston. I am expected."

"Please come in." His voice was low and husky as though he had a cold. He stood to one side and allowed her to enter. "This way."

He walked stiffly, woodenly, and with his dull expressionless eyes he reminded her of a film she had once seen about zombies. She shivered again and thrust the thought from her mind. He was probably the kindest of men; you couldn't judge by appearances.

Their footsteps echoed hollowly on the stone floor of the vast, cavernous hall with its wide oak staircase. Faded oil paintings of the Duval ancestors frowned down at her from the walls. A suit of armor stood on the wide landing at the top of the stairs.

As Ann glanced up she saw a quick flurry of movement as though someone had witnessed her arrival and then darted away, anxious not to be seen.

Then the butler was opening double wooden doors. "If you will wait in here please, m'amselle."

"Thank you."

The room was gloomy with dark-stained bookcases that reached almost to the ceiling. The shelves were dusty and filled with leatherbound volumes bearing faded gold lettering; they looked as though they had not been touched for years. There were dark velvet curtains and a large oak desk in one corner. A fire glowed in the large, old-fashioned fireplace, but the room was cold and smelt musty.

She was gazing up at a painting on the far wall when she heard a faint sound behind her. She half-turned quickly, catching her breath.

"I do apologize. I did not mean to startle you."

The man who stood beside the desk was smaller than Ann, with a gleaming, domelike head. He had a round, almost childlike face, with large, rubbery lips. He had very bushy brows, but it was his eyes which were his most outstanding feature; they were very large and wide. He was smiling, and he had one of the most seraphic smiles Ann had ever seen.

"I am Pierre Duval," he said and grasped her hand. His own hand was large and cold, and she had a feeling there was enormous strength in his fingers. "It was very good of you to come. Did you have a pleasant journey."

"Yes, I arrived yesterday. I'm staying with friends—the Langognes."

"Ah yes, the Langognes. I remember—" A violent clap of thunder interrupted him, followed by lingering rumbles. Rain like steel rods drove against the French windows.

"A dreadful day," he muttered. "I do hate storms, don't you, Ann?" His large eyes looked like those of a troubled child.

"They're certainly not very pleasant," she agreed.

"Well now, if you'll sit down and make yourself comfortable, my dear, I'll explain your duties to you. Then perhaps my wife will join us for coffee."

The Duvals, it seemed, had fingers in many pies, so Ann anticipated that the work would be interesting but not unduly arduous.

Duval got to his feet and drew the velvet curtains to escort Ann to the narrow doorway through which he had obviously come earlier. "This will be your office, Ann," he explained. "I trust you will find it satisfactory."

"It will do nicely," she said as she looked around the small square room. There was a typist's desk, a filing cabinet, and a smaller table on which stood a modern typewriter and a telephone. French windows overlooked the terrace and the rain-swept garden and lake. It was a pity, thought Ann, that the gardens had not been looked after; at one time it must have been a very lovely view.

"There's just one thing, my dear: I have no intercom. However, I've installed one of these—ah—buzzer contraptions, and I'll buzz for you when I want you. Otherwise you're not to disturb me, do you understand?"

"Yes, sir."

"Magnificent. Now, let me see, what else have I got to tell you?" He took a small slip of paper from his pocket. "My memory isn't what it used to be, I'm afraid. Ah yes—you are to meet my wife and later my daughter, Yvette."

Apart from the butler and the housekeeper-cook he told her there was no one else in the house. A maid came daily to help with the cooking and cleaning. Ann was to ring for tea or coffee at any time.

"You're very kind, monsieur."

"Not at all. You are to be one of the family." He smiled again, and she was somehow reminded of a smiling man on the plane. Constantly smiling men . . . she never did trust them. Yet Duval seemed very friendly and harmless enough.

"You're sure you won't find the work too much for you?"

"No, I'm sure it won't be."

"Good." He beamed at her happily. "We mustn't have you falling ill, must we? And your salary is adequate?" He sounded a little anxious.

"You've been very generous."

"Not at all. That was my wife's idea. She was very intent on employing an English girl."

Ann remembered Tom's conversation of the previous evening. He had told her that the local folk would not work at the chateau, and now she could understand why. The house was so dark and gloomy; she would be alone in her room for most of the day with no one to talk to. However, one couldn't have everything she decided philosophically and her salary was exceedingly generous.

It was ten minutes past eleven when a slim, rather sad-eyed maid tapped on the door and brought in a silver tray bearing three cups of coffee. She gave Ann a little curtsey and, after a quick and vaguely apprehensive glance at Duval, hurried out.

He shook his head. "Poor child. She suffers with bad nerves. Something to do with being born during the war—"

He broke off abruptly for the door had reopened and a middle-aged woman came slowly into the room, leaning heavily on a walking stick.

Juliette Duval had aged prematurely ever since the day when she learned of her son's sufferings in Dien Bien Phu. She was a dried-up little woman with sharp, angular features and thin, bloodless lips that drooped discontently at the corners. She wore a long black shawl over a severely cut black dress and the hand holding the stick was white-knuckled and bony. Her voice was sharp and high pitched.

Ann instantly decided that this quick-tempered, quick-tongued woman dominated her husband and everyone else in the household. For several seconds her cold eyes probed the girl—almost as though she were penetrating her flesh, trying to probe deeply into her mind.

"You are Ann Preston?"

"Yes, madame."

"From London?"

"Yes."

"Your father was a hunter—an explorer, I believe."

Ann was surprised at the question. "That's true, but I don't remember mentioning it to your agent in London."

"You didn't," said the bony-faced woman curtly. "We made enquiries about you. After all, there are many valuable objets d'art in the chateau. The Duval antiques have been here for generations."

Ann flushed but held her tongue. After all, she had to concede that it was not unusual for an employer to investigate a prospective employee's background. Nevertheless, there had been something vaguely offensive in the woman's voice.

"I understand," she murmured.

"You will not, of course, open any of the glass cabinets in order to examine their contents."

This time Ann could not keep a spark of anger from her eyes. "I wouldn't even dream of doing so!" she said.

"No?" The woman gave a twisted smile. "No, I don't think you would. Now for the things you *may* do. You may walk in the gardens when you wish, go swimming in the lake—"

"I'm afraid I can't swim, madame," Ann confessed.

"No? A pity. But there is a boat—you may amuse yourself with that if you wish. You may ring at any time for food and drink, and you have the complete freedom of the chateau to wonder about at your will."

"Thank you."

"With one exception, and that is the west wing . . ."

"Very well, madame, I—"

"Please let me continue," Juliette Duval interrupted sharply. "I will explain why. I wish there to be no mysteries, it is simply that the wing is falling into disrepair. One of these days when we have the money it will be demolished and rebuilt. But until then the staff are forbidden to use it. I do not want any accidents."

"I understand," said Ann.

"Very good. In that case, I am pleased to see you —very pleased indeed."

She turned and tapped her way out of the room. She was faintly smiling, but to Ann it seemed as though there was a peculiarly gloating look on the woman's face. It was a look Ann could find no way of accounting for, and presently she shrugged and put it from her mind.

Afterwards she was to remember it.

40

Chapter Four

It was still raining when Ann picked her way carefully down the muddy drive that evening. There was, she had been told, a bus at five-thirty which stopped at the crossroads, fifty yards from the chateau, which took the vineyard workers back to the village.

She knew that Peggy would be meeting her, but the sooner she got herself a little runabout the better, she thought. Perhaps Tom had been successful; she knew that he would try hard.

Her first day had not been particularly busy, and if it was an example of the work she had to do, she was surprised that Duval needed a permanent secretary. He could much more conveniently have employed a part-time typist from the village.

However, it was not her place to criticize. Perhaps there would be more work to come, when Duval had fully judged her capabilities.

Nevertheless, she was puzzled. Madame Duval's remark about the west wing had implied that there was little money to spare. Ann could not help wondering why, if economy was needed, Duval had gone to the expense of a full-time secretary.

Juliette Duval raised the corner of the net curtain in the large, comfortably furnished lounge on the second floor and watched Ann pick her way carefully round the puddles in the gravel drive. Then she dropped the curtain, reached for her stick which was leaning against the wall, and hobbled back to her chair beside the fire. She was a lover of the dark and rarely had the lights switched on. She sat there and gazed at the leaping flames which sent grotesque shadows dancing across the walls.

"It won't be long now, my dear," she murmured and gently patted the wicker basket beside her rocking chair. "It won't be long now," she repeated more loudly. And this time the basket began to creak, as though inhabited by some restless spirit.

Pierre Duval had been dozing in the deep chair on the other side of the huge fireplace, and now he stirred, rubbing his eyes and blinking in the gloom. There was a frown on his round smooth face.

"Did I hear the front door, Juliette?"

"It was only the girl."

"The girl?"

"Ann Preston!" she exclaimed impatiently.

"I was forgetting." He smiled, looked like a happy child. "I like her. She's kind and has good manners. She reminds me of my youth, of a girl I once knew. Do you remember?"

"As if I could ever forget! I thought we had agreed not to talk of her again?"

"I'm sorry. I forgot. I'm growing old—so are you."

"You don't have to remind me!" She almost spat the words.

He sighed, as though heavy with memories. "I wish she could stay here; its nice to have her around. Besides, there is such a lot of work to do." He paused, then went on peevishly: "She should live in. After all, I am her employer!"

"Of course you are, Pierre. You should insist."

"But I don't like to—"

"You must, my Pierre." Her voice was kinder now. "As you have said, you *are* her employer."

He got to his feet, nodding his head slowly, his eyes vacant, his movements jerky, rather like a puppet on a string. Then he said, "Did you notice that smell in here today?"

"Smell? What sort of smell?"

"Lilies of the valley and dead leaves," he said, his voice almost a whisper.

She stared at him. His eyes were unnaturally bright, and she sighed deeply as she noticed. She knew the signs. As though she hadn't enough trouble! But when she answered him her voice was still gentle.

"Why don't you go and amuse yourself, Pierre?"

He nodded absently. "I think I will. Do you think there will be a full moon tonight?"

"Yes, I think so, my Pierre."

"I do like a nice moon," he said, smiling happily.

He went out, and the door closed quietly behind him. The woman sat staring deeply into the heart of the flames. It was almost as though she were waiting for something. Then, quite suddenly, she heard the distant sound of music, an orchestra playing softly. It came from the library, the room below.

The music grew louder, rising to a crescendo, its throbbing beat resounding in her blood. It was an old tune, a tune she knew by heart. She waited expectantly, rigid in her chair, her hands gripping the wooden arms like a vice.

Then it came, that dreadful, bloodcurdling sound she had heard so many times before; shrilling, bubbling, maniacal laughter that echoed and reechoed through the long dark corridors of the old chateau.

Vague stirrings came from the wicker basket beside Juliette Duval's chair.

"It's all right," she whispered soothingly. "It's nothing to worry about, my dear. . . ."

A surprise awaited Ann just outside the huge wrought-iron gates. The car there was not Peggy's familiar green Renault, but a low-slung sports model with a long black hood. Ann's heart leapt as she recognized the man behind the steering wheel.

"Steve!"

"Hi! Hop in."

"But I'm expecting Peggy at any moment." She felt very wet and bedraggled and very self-conscious as she gazed down into his grinning features.

"She's not coming; I've fixed it with her. Jump in, Ann; you'll get soaked to the skin."

She slid into the passenger seat beside him. The car smelt warm and leathery; the windshield wipers ticked back and forth with a reassuring sound.

"I called on Peggy this afternoon," Steve explained as the car moved off down the lane.

Ann was surprised. She removed her scarf and shook out her blonde hair. "How do you know her?"

"I don't—or rather, I didn't until this afternoon. But she's very charming, and I've always wanted to meet her. She has quite a reputation in the States. I explained that we'd met on the plane coming over and suggested that I call for you when you left work."

"She was probably glad of the offer," said Ann. "I know she's terribly busy. I feel like such a nuisance. I'm hoping to get a car of my own soon."

"So Peggy was saying. But until then I'll be only too pleased to be of service."

"It's very kind of you, but—"

"It's my pleasure."

"Well, we'll see," Ann conceded. "What's your hotel like?"

"Not bad, considering."

"Have you begun your research yet? You know, on the book."

He glanced into the rear mirror and drove away. "Started last night. I had a lucky break. I ran into Yvette Duval, and she's offered to help me. She knows most of the chateaux around here."

"I see." Ann thought that if Tom were to be believed Yvette had her own motives for wanting to assist Steve Martin. She had gathered from Duval that his daughter was not at the chateau, and she wondered where she had gone after leaving the club the previous evening.

"But don't let's talk about me," Steve said. "How did you get on today?"

"Fine, thanks."

"Keep you busy?"

"Far from it. It's a rest compared to the hectic time in my old London office."

He frowned. "Seems a bit odd, doesn't it? I mean, getting a girl from England to fill the job?"

"Haven't you heard the saying that the best secretaries are English?" asked Ann with a smile. "They go mad over them in the States, apparently. Still, I must admit the idea did occur to me. I expect there's quite a simple explanation: it's probably just as difficult to get office staff here as it is in London."

"What are the Duvals like?" he asked.

"It's difficult to say at this stage. I've only met them both for a few minutes. But he seemed quite friendly; in fact, they both were, I suppose."

"You sound a little dubious," he said. He rubbed his chin. "I don't think Peggy is too happy about your working there. She seems to think the old man—Pierre Duval—is a bit off."

"I'm sure he isn't. You know how rumors spread, stemming from the most stupid things."

"There's no smoke without fire," he muttered. "I'd be very careful if I were you, Ann."

"Oh, really!" she exclaimed.

His expression was grim. "Look, I've been talking to some of the locals, and they believe the rumors. No one will work there. Why a man was killed at the chateau only a few weeks ago."

Ann was startled. "What?"

"Some masonry fell on him in the west wing. And last year a man was found drowned in the lake. The place has a curse on it."

She laughed a little uneasily. "Nonsense! I don't believe in that kind of talk. Anyway, I've been warned not to go into the west wing. Madame told me that it was dangerous, and that they didn't want any accidents." As she spoke she found herself wondering why the woman had not said "any *more* accidents." But perhaps she had not wanted to frighten her, or dwell on the unhappy incident.

"I see." Steve looked thoughtful. Then he shot her a quick glance. "You're shivering. Are you cold?"

"No," she said. Then, with a smile: "But perhaps I'm catching one." It was silly, but suddenly the thought of Juliette Duval with her yellow, witchlike face, had sent a cold shudder down her spine. However, she was not prepared to admit it to Steve.

As though sensing her trend of thought he suddenly said, "What's she like—Juliette Duval?"

"She's a smallish woman, and I think she could be pretty acid-tongued if the occasion arose.

But she said she hoped I would be happy there. She's given me the run of the place."

"That's interesting."

"Interesting?" She was puzzled at the tone of his voice.

"Oh, nothing." He shrugged. "Perhaps I should have said, 'That's fine.' After all, you don't want to be restricted to one room, day in and day out, do you? But mind you don't run into the ghost."

She laughed. "I'll tell you if I do."

"Is that a promise?"

"Why, yes—but I don't suppose I'll have to keep it."

"You never know," he muttered. "There's something very queer about the place—the way there is about all these spooky old buildings."

Ann felt a momentary irritation. "You and Peggy are both the same; you keep trying to make out there's something sinister there! It's simply that it's old and dark and rather gloomy, but the people seem friendly enough . . . though I haven't met Yvette yet," she added. "What's she like?"

"She seemed quite pleasant. I found her a little self-centered, but otherwise I quite liked her."

For the second time in twenty-four hours Ann felt a quick stab of jealousy. "Then I won't bother to get you an invitation to the chateau," she said, with a faint note of irony in her voice. "She'll probably invite you herself."

"I hope so. If she does I'll make a bee-line for your office. Where is it, by the way?"

"On the ground floor, adjoining the library," she told him.

"The library? Is that where Duval works?"

"Yes."

"I must remember that," he said. "I wouldn't want to visit the chateau and not see you."

The car began to slow. They had reached the village now; it looked gray in the falling rain. The *patisserie* was closed; the Café des Sports was empty save for a bearded man sitting in the corner against the window. He looked vaguely like the man who had smiled at her on the plane, Ann thought. A young woman emerged from the little graveyard further up the street; she was weeping and there was something familiar about her too. The graveyard was full of moss-covered stones, dank grass, weeds, dead and dying flowers.

As the gate clanged shut behind the girl and as she passed the car, Ann recognized her as Marie, the maid she had seen at the chateau. Now she thought she knew the reason for the girl's sad eyes.

Ann arrived punctually at nine o'clock the following morning to find enough work on her desk to keep her busy for weeks. She was pleased rather than dismayed, for she would rather be busy than sitting down doing nothing.

Before she started working she remembered the night before. He had waited for her while she changed, and then they had driven into the village. The Continentale proved to be a small but cozy place, and the meal was superb. They had gone on from there to a club and had danced until two in the morning, when Ann had reluctantly decided she must leave to be fit for work in the morning, reluctant because it meant leaving the warm, exciting nearness of the man who was beginning to mean so much to her.

She had enjoyed every moment of her evening with Steve. He was gay and interesting, with a sense of humor which matched her own, widely traveled too, with a store of anecdotes that he related graphically, and often with wit. He had been born in Manhattan, the son of a stockbroker who had sent him to England to be educated. After college Steve had, to the dismay of his parents, joined the Merchant Marines—deciding that it was the best and cheapest way to see the world. Meeting up with a New York journalist in Miami, he had been fired with the ambition to write— which he had done quite successfully; his success had enabled him to live in Denmark.

In return Ann told him something of herself, of the terrible day when her father had been killed.

"At the time it seemed as though the world had come to an end," she said. "I worshiped my father. He was a man who loved giving, especially surprises. Living with him was an adventure in itself." She paused. "I wonder why the best people always go first. Have you noticed that, Steve?"

He nodded. "It doesn't make much sense, does it?"

"I don't know what I'd have done without Peggy. It wasn't easy for her. She was married to a man who was one of life's failures and knew it; he drank excessively because of his sense of failure, and he was very rarely home. There were times, I think, when she just didn't know how to make ends meet."

"You and Tom must have been very close," he said.

"We were. He was always gentle and sympathetic."

"And now?"

She flushed without replying.

"All right," he smiled. "You don't have to tell me. He's in love with you; that's understandable enough. Are you in love with him?"

She hesitated, then shook her head. She didn't know why she was telling him all this, unless it was because he was just the kind of man who invited confidences.

"No," she said. "I'm not in love with him. I like him—enormously. But that isn't love, is it?"

His eyes clouded. "No." For a moment there was sadness in the depths of his voice, and his lips were compressed. Then he was laughing. "We're here to have fun, so let's have it," he said, and whirled her onto the floor.

Afterwards, when he brought her home, he had kissed her. He had murmured soft endearments into her ear, caressed her hair. And she had clung to him, filled with a happiness she had never believed possible. For both of them it had been love at first sight, something she had always scornfully rejected as impossible—until now.

If only it hadn't meant hurting Tom! She felt sure he had guessed; her flushed cheeks and sparkling eyes had given her away. And hurting Tom was the last thing she wanted to do. . . .

She pulled herself together. This was no time to indulge in sentiment; there was work to be done.

She was hard at it when Marie came in with her coffee. She looked tired, and Ann wondered who she had been mourning for in the churchyard the previous evening.

"M'sieu Duval wondered if you would like cognac with your coffee, miss?" said Marie hesitantly.

"No thank you, Marie, though it was kind of

him to suggest it. And, please—won't you call me Ann?"

The girl colored. "Thank you, m'amselle—I mean, Ann."

"Don't go," said Ann trying to put the girl at her ease. "I get a little lonely here on my own. You come in daily, don't you?"

"Yes, but I would not spend one single night in this chateau." There was sudden vehemence in the girl's voice.

"Oh? Why not?" asked Ann.

"Have you not heard?" The girl's eyes were large and round. "It is haunted!"

Ann stirred her coffee and smiled faintly. "Oh, come now, Marie. Surely you don't really believe that?"

"But yes!" The maid looked at her almost indignantly. "It is not the question of believing, but of seeing."

"Seeing what?"

"I have seen it. It was young M'sieu Gaston! It was terrible! And the smell . . ."

"Smell?" repeated Ann, sharply now.

The maid nodded her head vigorously. "Yes. Like flowers—lilies of the valley—and something else. Something nasty and decaying. It made me feel quite sick. He was staring straight at me; his lips were moving, but I could hear nothing. I saw only that awful, twisted face! *Mon Dieu*," she finished in a whisper. "I shall never forget it." She suddenly leaned forward and clutched Ann's arm. "I tell you, I have seen it, I swear to you."

"I believe you if you say so, Marie," Ann said soothingly. She could see that the girl, highly strung and obviously imaginative, was distressed. Quickly she changed the subject. "Didn't I see you yesterday evening, coming out of the cemetery?"

The girl glanced quickly toward the door as though afraid of being overheard. Then she murmured: "I go there once a week to burn the candle . . . for Jacques."

"Who is—was Jacques?"

"But of course, you would not know. He was the gardener here." Marie looked away. "We were going to be married this year, and then . . ." Her voice faltered and her eyes filled with tears.

"Don't tell me if it upsets you," Ann said softly.

"But I must, m'amselle!" Marie said fiercely. "It must be a warning to you. It happened just after eleven o'clock one morning. He goes to trim the roses against the wall of the west wing. Then—*mon Dieu!*—there comes a terrible rumbling noise, and Jacques cry out!" She suddenly covered her eyes with her hands and began to sob. "It was the battlements. Part of them had collapsed. And Jacques, he was buried."

"Oh, Marie, I am so sorry!" said Ann.

The girl raised tear-stained eyes. "When they

come from the village with the . . . the bulldozer, they find him. He was holding a red rose in his hand. But that is not the end. The men, they gave me the rose; they said he must have been picking it for me. We were very much in love . . . but when Yvette hear about it, she take it from me and toss it in the kitchen stove. She say it is sick to keep things that remind one of the dead, one must live for the living."

Ann said nothing. She would visualize only too clearly the scene Marie had described: the cruel Yvette, snatching the rose from Marie and flinging it into the fire, the leaves curling, the stem splitting open, the sap sizzling, the petals charring to black cinders. Why had she done such a heartless thing?

"She kept saying it is morbid to cling to the past, morbid and sick." Marie clenched her fists until the knuckles showed white; her eyes glowed in her pallid face. "I hate her!" she shouted suddenly. "I hate her! One of these days I will get even with her. She robbed me. Now I have nothing, *nothing!*"

"You mustn't talk like that." Ann slipped her arm around the distraught girl. "Hate destroys, don't you know that?"

The girl swung round, her lips quivering. "You're kind, but they are not. They are warped, twisted, mad! Don't stay here, Ann! Get a job somewhere else. They'll destroy you! They feast on misery and despair! Get out while you can!"

"Oh, Marie—" Ann began.

"Listen!" The girl interrupted her fiercely. "They're all as bad as each other. And him, with his friendly smile, his gentle voice—he's worse than any of them; he is the *crazy* one. Oh go, please go—while there is still time!" Sobbing, she flung herself from the room.

Chapter Five

Ann lit a cigarette and stared at the closed door. The Duval family might be a little odd, she reflected, but people did tend to become eccentric when they lived lonely lives. But that didn't necessarily make them mad.

Poor Marie. Her grief must be eating away inside her like some razor-toothed bug, robbing her of logical thought. What else could explain her wild outburst, directed against her employers? If there was any truth in her assertion that the chateau was evil, haunted, even dangerous, why did she remain there? And only a mind unbalanced by grief could hold the Duvals responsible for the accident to the gardener—although nothing, she thought, could excuse Yvette's subsequent callousness in the matter of the rose.

Ann finished her coffee and her cigarette and began typing again. Soon afterwards Pierre Duval came in; if he had overheard Marie's outburst, he gave no sign. The stem of his pipe clenched between his teeth, his face wreathed in a friendly smile, he fumbled in the pocket of his dressing gown for matches.

"And how are you this morning, Ann?" he asked in his soft, husky voice. "Well? Splendid!" He hesitated, then gave a helpless little shrug of his shoulders. "Because . . . well, oh dear, there is something I must say, and I don't know how to say it."

"Is there something wrong with my work, M'sieu Duval?" Ann asked quickly.

"No, no!" He raised his hands in mock horror. "I am foolish, am I not? I don't know how to express myself properly; your language is so difficult."

She smiled. "Both you and Madame Duval speak English very well indeed, m'sieu. But what is bothering you? I wish you'd tell me."

He took a deep breath and looked at her as though coming to a decision.

"As you have probably gathered from the correspondence here, I have three partners, yes?" And when she nodded: "Marcel—he is the senior director and a most ambitious man. Work, that is all he thinks about. Well, he has been on the telephone this morning—always in this terrible haste, he is. 'Please,' he says to me. 'It is no good!' 'What is no good, my old friend?' I say. 'Your annual stock lists. Head office has not received them.' *Mon Dieu!*" The little man looked suitably aghast. "All I can say is that he is right. I have forgotten. Can you understand that, Ann?"

She smiled, amused at his concern. "We all forget things at times, particularly if the pressure is on."

He nodded eagerly. "I knew you would understand. Since Helene, my previous secretary, left my employ to have a baby, the whole organization has gone to pieces. Marcel, he is nearly going crazy! 'Are you a fool?' he booms over the telephone. 'Are you an imbecile? Are you trying to destroy us?' It will be done, I say. My new secretary will cope with the matter." He paused and looked at her a little anxiously.

Again she smiled, and nodded. "You want me to work late, of course? I shall be only too pleased."

"Ah, that is good!" He looked relieved. "I knew you would be most helpful. I will tell my wife to arrange for a bedroom to be prepared."

Ann was startled. "A bedroom?" she stammered, with sudden recollection of all the warnings which had been drummed into her over the last day or two.

"But of course," he said, a note of surprise in his voice. "Did I not make myself clear? You will have to work very late, very often. Much will depend on when the various agents submit the lists from the warehouses, here and abroad. Immediately they arrive they must be copied and despatched to the head office."

Ann bit her lip. She couldn't very well refuse, although she certainly did not want to spend tonight—or any night—in this gloomy old house. Besides, it meant that she would be unable to see Steve . . . again she remembered Marie's warnings, then shrugged them off. Nonsense! She counted herself a good judge of character, and there was something rather nice, even a little pathetic, about Pierre Duval. What possible harm could he do her?

"I'm most terribly sorry," Duval went on quickly. "It is unavoidable, and of course I am to blame. Juliette will be furious. She can be most difficult. It will only take a few days at the outside, and I do assure you, you will be most welcome to stay here."

Ann resigned herself philosophically to the idea. She would be sorry not to see Steve, but it couldn't be helped. There would be plenty of other opportunities. And in a way it would solve a problem; she had foreseen that there would be difficulties, even embarrassment, living under the same roof as Tom, knowing how he felt about her.

"Very well, M'sieu Duval," she agreed. "But I shall have to go home first, to collect a few things."

It was dark when Ann arrived back at the chateau, and she was grateful that the bus driver considerately dropped her off outside the wrought-iron gates.

"Sooner you than me, m'amselle," he grunted as she alighted.

The other passengers had huddled together and whispered and eyed her covertly when she had asked for the chateau. But she supposed there was nothing unnatural in that. It was the same in any country village in Britain or, for that matter, in the world. Strangers have always been the subject of conversation and speculation, and no doubt it was well known that she was the new English secretary.

The drive seemed darker than ever, and there were strange rustlings in the undergrowth as night creatures with beady eyes paused in their scavenging to watch her, tensed to vanish if she made a suspicious move in their direction. Skeletal-like boughs swayed eerily as the breeze rustled through the leaves.

She walked around the side of the chateau and let herself in with the back-door key that Duval had given her. The kitchen was in darkness, which accentuated the red glow of the stove. The room smelt warm and homely, of freshly baked bread, and it reminded her of her childhood when she had played in Peggy's kitchen.

As Ann stepped through the communicating door into the cavernous hall, Juliette Duval came down the oak staircase. "You quite startled me, my dear!" she said.

"I'm sorry," Ann replied. "I didn't mean to."

"Of course you didn't. Have you had anything to eat?" And when Ann told her that she had: "Good. Now you must look upon the chateau as your home." She gave a peculiar smile as she tapped her way into the hall. "You are one of the family now, you know."

"You're very kind," said Ann. The words were kind, but she sensed a falseness behind them, an insincerity. But then she mentally reprimanded herself for the ungraciousness of her thoughts.

Juliette Duval drew her long black shawl more closely about her shoulders. "Not at all," she said. "You've been good enough to give up your evenings to work here. But, do come in, Pierre has been worried for you. I have too, of course. I would never forgive myself if anything happened to you. Yvette has just arrived. It's a change for her to be here at all, although it is where she belongs. She should love it as I do!" Her voice rose accusingly.

"You forget, you are getting old," Duval's voice suddenly was heard, "and Yvette is young."

His wife's eyes widened. "Don't keep reminding me, Pierre," she said icily. "A good daughter's place is in her home."

"Papa is right," a raised voice came from the lounge. "This is no place for a young girl. Live here and die young—and I mean that in every way."

"Be quiet!" Juliette's voice was shrill.

"It's true," came the sulky reply. "I don't know why you want to—"

"You've said enough, Yvette!" It was almost a hiss. Juliette's face was white and strained, her lips tightly compressed. "We have company. What will M'amselle Preston think of us quarreling?"

"Why conceal it?" Yvette's voice sounded bored. "If she stays with us long enough she will soon realize what we're like—that we get on each others' nerves, that we've nothing in common— except the precious name of Duval."

Juliette's eyes were bright with anger now, her nostrils pinched. With an effort she forced a smile.

"My daughter is always—how you say, difficult? Pay her no mind."

Yvette was sprawled full length on a settee drawn up before the fire in the lounge. Her raven-black hair flowed loosely about her shoulders and a cigarette drooped from her scarlet lips. She wore a tight-fitting orange sweater and purple slacks. Her lovely eyes appraised Ann coolly but her greeting was friendly enough.

"Welcome, Ann." Her smile faded and she frowned. "Haven't I seen you somewhere before?"

"I was at the same club you were in the other night."

"Of course! I remember now. You were with Tom Langogne . . . nice but boring."

"I wouldn't say that." Ann sprang quickly to Tom's defense.

"Don't tell me you're in love with him?" said Yvette with an amused expression.

"No, of course not. But he is a very old friend. We were brought up together."

Yvette looked bored. "Well, you certainly get around, considering you haven't been here very long," she said.

Ann felt her temper rise at something in the other girl's voice. "I don't know what you mean," she said, with sudden asperity.

"Last night it was Steve Martin, wasn't it? Another old friend?"

"I'm sure that what I do on my own time is my own affair," said Ann coldly.

"But of course it is!" beamed Pierre Duval, sensing the sudden antagonism between his daughter and his new secretary. "And why shouldn't Miss Preston enjoy her evenings? She is young.

Now, if you will permit us, we have much work to do."

He patted Ann's hand affectionately as they entered her office.

"Take no notice of my daughter. She is the difficult one, perhaps because we have spoilt her. Besides, I think she likes the American who has come to the village." He shot her a quick glance. "You know him well?"

Ann shook her head. "We only met on the plane coming from England."

"I see." Duval looked thoughtful, his round smooth face was creased in a frown. "I wonder . . . oh, it doesn't matter."

"Is something bothering you?" asked Ann.

He spread his hands and shrugged. "Well . . . I was wondering if he knew the other two Americans who have rented a villa outside the village. I hope not for your sake because I do not like them. Once or twice I have fancied I have seen the bearded one hanging about in the lane."

"Bearded?" Ann stiffened, remembering the bearded man she had seen in the Café des Sports. "Did he have thick, black-rimmed spectacles?"

"Why, yes. Do you know him?"

"He also was on the plane and spoke to me once or twice. But what makes you think he is 'hanging about' here, M'sieu Duval? What reason would he have?"

Duval brushed tobacco ash from his jacket. "Who knows? Perhaps I should inform the police. As you know, we have many objets d'art here. However," he beamed at her again, "you must not bother your pretty head about it. You have enough to do. Later I will bring you a hot drink and sandwiches." With a friendly nod he went out, quietly closing the door behind him.

How on earth could anybody say he was mad, thought Ann. He could be very charming—and he had been quick to perceive Yvette's antagonism. A little eccentric he might be perhaps, but he was certainly not mad.

Yvette? Ann suspected she had made an enemy there. The girl was obviously spoiled and used to having her own way. And she was undoubtedly resentful of Ann's friendship with Steve Martin. Well, if she thought she could take Steve from her, just let her try!

Suddenly Ann wrinkled her nostrils, conscious of a not unpleasant scent which filled the room, as though not long before someone had been in there, someone who used a fragrant perfume. It was unmistakably not Yvette's for her scent was almost overpowering, and Juliette, she had noticed, used none at all.

Ann caught her breath. Lilies of the valley! The scent which was always associated with the ghost of the dead son! Icy fingers closed around her heart, and she felt a moment of panic, an urge to rush quickly from the room. Then she got a grip on herself.

Don't be a little fool! she told herself fiercely. Ghosts! You must be out of your mind! You've been listening to too much talk, the product of Marie's overfertile mind!

She sat down behind her typewriter, fumbling in her handbag for cigarettes. She lit up, inhaling deeply, expelling a steady stream of white tobacco smoke from her mouth. That was better. There was nothing like a cigarette.

She got up, walked around the room. No, the strange perfume was no longer there; it had gone as mysteriously as it had come. Perhaps it had never been there in the first place. Ghosts don't exist, except in the imagination.

She went back to her desk and began to work. She worked until ten, when Duval returned with hot milk and sandwiches. He seemed pleased with the progress she had made and told her he had no wish to overwork her; she could be done for that night.

"You look tired, my dear." His eyes were concerned, his voice gentle. "It has been a long day. Juliette is about to retire, and she will show you to your room when you are ready."

However, because it took Ann time to finish up what she was doing, it was Yvette who escorted

Ann up the wide oak staircase to a long dark corridor on the third floor.

"I must apologize for my behavior earlier," she said to Ann surprisingly. "I didn't mean to be rude; it's just my way. Will you forgive me?"

"Of course," said Ann, instantly warming toward her. "I'd forgotten about it already."

"Steven is very nice. I'm going to help him with his research."

"So he told me. I'm sure he will appreciate it."

"He's quite different from the type of men I'm used to meeting in Paris. They are—how do you call it, arty-craft? All they do is talk about writing and painting, but they never *do* anything! For him, I would do anything. I would fight for a man like that."

Was there a threat in the words, a warning? Ann couldn't be sure. Yvette opened a door halfway down the long dark passage, and then she leaned in and touched a switch.

"Here is your room."

It was large, with faded wallpaper and a threadbare carpet on the floor. A chandelier was suspended from the cracked ceiling by a long chain, but there were only two low-powered bulbs in the sockets, so much of the room was in darkness.

"I'm afraid it is not very well furnished," Yvette apologized. "Times have changed . . . and we don't entertain any more."

"Don't worry, I shall be quite all right," Ann said. She waited until the other girl had gone, then looked around the room. The wardrobe and dressing table were old and eaten up with woodworms; her case had been placed on a rickety chair next to a single bed which looked as though it had come out of the ark. The room itself was cold, and rain spattered against the windows.

It was certainly not the last word in comfort! Ann turned the key in the lock, which she noticed was fairly new, and undressed.

She was surprised to find that she did not feel particularly tired and wondered if it was because the room was cold. Or perhaps it was that she was unwilling to put out the lights. The house was so quiet, with a stillness that seemed to invade her whole being, as though something evil and malignant watched and waited for darkness to fill the rooms.

She shivered and lit a cigarette, aware that her fingers were shaking. What on earth was the matter with her? Normally her nerves were rock-steady. She supposed that she was just overtired, and that all she had been told about the Duvals and the old chateau was now crowding her thoughts. The ghost of Gaston Duval, the strange scent of lilies of the valley, Marie's frightened eyes as she warned her not to stay in the house—all these combined were not at all calculated to make her feel at ease.

She was behaving like a frightened schoolgirl, she told herself angrily. What possible harm could come to her? The door was locked, she had locked it before she started to undress.

Hadn't she?

Doubts began to assail her. She couldn't remember. Surely it was the first thing she would do, wasn't it? Better make sure, though . . .

She padded across the worn carpet—and then her heart gave a sudden violent lurch. She froze at the door, her mouth open, her eyes wide and startled.

Someone was outside the room—turning the door handle . . .

Chapter Six

Ann's mouth was dry; she felt paralyzed and could hardly breathe. She stared almost hypnotically as the door handle began to turn the other way, as though whoever was outside the door had realized it was locked.

Certainly this was no ghost! And the thought gave Ann courage.

"Who's there?" she called sharply.

She heard a muffled gasp and then the soft patter of running footsteps. Swiftly she opened the door and ran into the dark passage. She was just in time to see a shadowy figure disappear into a second corridor which ran at right angles to her own. She turned into it, and as she raced in pursuit she caught a flurry of movement at the far end of the corridor as the door at the end of it slammed shut.

Then the door on her right opened and a man came out, barring her way. He exclaimed in astonishment, "M'amselle Preston! What is it? What is the matter?" It was Raymonde, the gaunt-faced butler. He wore a long dressing gown over his pajamas, and there was a pipe in his hand.

"Somebody tried to get into my room!" she said breathlessly.

He raised a bushy eyebrow and looked skeptical. "I find that difficult to believe, m'amselle. There's no one else on this floor apart from myself. You must have been dreaming."

"Don't be ridiculous!" she said sharply. "I hadn't gone to sleep. Anyway, I know quite well I saw somebody. Whoever it was, disappeared through that door at the far end."

"*Mon Dieu*, that is impossible! It leads to the west wing. It is most dangerous beyond that door. The floorboards are crumbling away. It would be doubly dangerous in the dark!"

"Well, that's the way he went," said Ann stubbornly.

A dark flush suffused the butler's sunken features, then he shrugged. "If you will wait a moment, please, I will get a light. I will show you."

He went into his room and returned with a large chromium torch, then led the way down the corridor and opened the door. In the light of the torch which he played about the room beyond, Ann saw the jagged edges of holes where the rotting floorboards had given way. Plaster had crumbled from the walls to reveal patches of damp brickwork, and cobwebs hung from the blackened beams. There was a sour smell of decay.

"It would be practically impossible for anyone to run through here in the dark, as you can see," the butler said, in his husky, throaty voice.

Ann turned away, suddenly conscious of the fact that she was wearing only her pajamas. Whoever the intruder had been, he would be well away by this time.

"I must have been mistaken," she confessed, as he closed the door, cutting off the icy draft. "I'm sorry." But she was quite convinced in her own mind that she had not imagined it.

"It is nothing, m'amselle . . . a strange house. Please do not hesitate to call me if anything else should disturb you." He gave a stiff little bow, went back into his room and closed the door.

Ann hurried back to her own room and locked it again. Whatever Raymonde said to the contrary, she was convinced that somebody had tried to open her door, and had fled to the west wing when she ran in pursuit. But who?

She fell asleep still wondering. . . .

When she awoke pale watery sunshine was filtering through the dust-covered window. The world outside looked gray and uninviting, the dark clouds blowing across the sky.

She had breakfast with Juliette Duval in the

cold, cheerless dining room. The thin-lipped woman made no mention of her husband but said that Yvette was still in bed.

"She is lazy, that one," she said peevishly. "Not like my son was. . . ." Ann saw her eyes soften. "You will have been told that my son, Gaston, was killed in Dien Bien Phu?"

"Yes," said Ann. "I am very sorry."

"A brave man . . . they did such terrible things to him. Wars are so senseless! So many hearts are broken . . . but, always, he will live on in my heart, you understand? I will never let him die—never!" There was something in her eyes, in the vehemence of her voice, that sent a sudden shiver down Ann's spine. She was glad she could excuse herself to start work.

It was a long and busy morning. The dwarflike Pierre Duval brought in another batch of work, but apart from some generalities about the weather, he said nothing. He looked tired, and there was a glassiness about his eyes which had not been there the day before. He was morose and preoccupied and had not even bothered to shave.

Ann hoped that either Tom or Steve—Steve preferably—would have telephoned her, but the phone had remained silent; she had been left very much on her own. It was lonely having no one to speak to, to break the monotony.

She was told that she could have lunch in her

office, and she gratefully accepted. Afterwards she retired to her bedroom for an hour, filled with determination. The Duvals always rested after lunch, and she knew that Raymonde was enjoying an after-lunch glass of wine in the cook's quarters.

Her curiosity had been aroused by the events of the previous night, and she meant to satisfy it, if possible. The more she thought about it, the more she suspected that Raymonde had been trying to put her off the scent.

The house was silent as she made her way along the corridor. The door leading to the west wing was still unlocked, and that in itself was intriguing: If the rooms beyond were so dangerous, why wasn't the door kept locked?

She switched on her flashlight and carefully skirted the holes in the floorboards as she picked her way across the room. The next door led to a second corridor littered with fallen plaster and brick rubble. It was cold and damp—and very drafty because several window panes were missing; dust and cobwebs were everywhere.

The rooms were unfurnished and had fallen into complete disrepair—so that the final room at the end of the corridor came as a shock. She stood staring into it, her pulse quickening with excitement as she took in the implications of what she saw.

An attempt had been made to make this room comfortable! There was a warm-looking carpet on the floor and thick blue curtains at the windows. Two deep easy chairs were on either side of a glowing oil stove. There were books piled on a table beside a bed covered with a silken eiderdown, and newspapers and magazines littered the floor. Tins of food and drink stood on the shelves of a white cupboard.

So she had not been mistaken. Someone was actually living here in the west wing!

As she stood there a framed photograph on the small table beside the bed caught her eye. She walked across and picked it up. It was a head-and-shoulder picture of a pretty girl with a round, attractive face and derisive, mocking eyes. Her shapely lips were curved in a wide smile, revealing very square white teeth. Ann could almost hear her light infectious laugh—a girl who bubbled with vitality, a girl who would be teasing, provocative, mysterious—

Suddenly she stiffened, feeling the skin prickle at the back of her neck. Once more she had that sensation of being watched by somebody—somebody both evil and malignant.

She spun around. There was nobody in the doorway, but the feeling persisted. Swiftly replacing the photograph, Ann hurried out of the room. It was time she left anyway, she reflected; it wouldn't be pleasant being found there by the occupier—whoever he was. Or had he already seen her, been watching her?

And who was he? Was the Duval family aware of his existence? They must surely be. The wing would be inspected periodically. Besides, there were the cans of food. Somebody must be supplying the occupant of the room with food and drink.

No sooner had Ann reached her office than the telephone jangled. She picked it up.

"Ann Preston?" she said crisply.

"Ann? This is Steve," came his friendly voice.

"Oh, Steve, how wonderful to hear from you!" She could not keep the pleasure from her voice.

"Are you all right?" He sounded anxious.

"Of course!"

"That's good. I was worried—"

"You don't have to be. I'm quite happy, but very busy."

"Oh." There was no mistaking his disappointment, and the knowledge gave her a little thrill. "So you don't think there's any chance of my being able to see you?"

"Not for a day or two, I'm afraid," she admitted reluctantly.

He said something softly beneath his breath, then went on: "Listen, Ann, I'm not moving far from the hotel, so if you want me . . ."

"Bless you, Steve. You're very sweet. But there's really nothing to worry about. Have you been busy?"

She could almost see the shake of his head, the wry smile. "No, just relaxing and soaking up atmosphere. By the way, there's been some excitement in the village."

"Excitement? What kind of excitement?"

"A girl has been attacked."

"Good heavens! Is she all right?"

"Yes, although she was taken to hospital suffering from shock . . . so please be careful, darling, if you go for a walk on the grounds."

She was touched by his concern. "I will," she promised. "But you don't think whoever did it is lurking near the chateau, do you?"

"You can't be too certain. Anyone could hide in that overgrown wilderness. . . ." There was a pause and she could hear the sound of his breathing. Then: "I miss you, Ann."

"I miss you too," she said.

"I'd wangle an invitation to the chateau, but I haven't seen Yvette. Is she there?"

"Yes, but I don't know exactly where at the moment."

"Perhaps I could phone her?"

"Of course. Now I think I'd better hang up; I've so much to do."

"All right. I'll be thinking of you, Ann—and anxiously waiting for the time when I can see you again."

She felt a lump rise into her throat. "That makes two of us. Goodbye, Steve."

She replaced the receiver and leaned back in her chair. Her face was warm, her eyes starry. He had sounded so concerned—and he had called her darling! It was wonderful to be cared for. . . .

Upstairs, lying on her bed, her hand still on the extension, Yvette stared savagely at the ceiling, her eyes smoldering with fury.

"So that's the way it is, is it?" she muttered as she gently replaced the receiver. "Well. we'll have to do something about it, won't we, Ann, *darling?*"

Ann found it difficult to concentrate on work that afternoon. For one thing, she could not forget the caress in Steve's voice, and she longed to see him again. She wondered if he would telephone Yvette in the hope of receiving an invitation to the chateau so that he could see Ann—not that she approved of deceit; she was disturbed because she knew that the French girl would use every weapon in her power to steal Steve from her.

The second reason for her lack of concentration was the discovery of the furnished room in the west wing. Who was there? And who was supplying him with provisions? Raymonde?

Certainly the butler's appearance had been timely; it had prevented her from following the flying figure to his ultimate destination, had enabled him to get away.

She wondered what Steve would make of it all when she told him. Until then she must try to thrust the incident from her mind; there was just too much to do. . . .

It was late afternoon, just after she had drawn the curtains and switched on the light, when she heard the music. It came from the adjoining library, an old French tune she remembered from her childhood. Unfortunately the tune was not much played these days, she thought, this being the age of rock music. It was a sad, nostalgic tune, enhanced by the strings and the haunting wail of a saxophone.

Duval must have started work and was playing background music. Ann enjoyed it, providing it wasn't too loud, and she began to hum softly to herself as she checked the list she had just typed.

Suddenly she jumped and winced, for the volume had been turned up, and now the record was harsh and discordant, the waves of sound beating against the communicating door. It hammered at her eardrums, almost deafening her.

She put her hands to her ears, grimacing, trying to shut out the cacophonic sounds. It was impossible to concentrate. When she thought the record had ended, she withdrew her hands, and soon realized it was being replayed with the volume turned down.

Heaving a sigh of relief, she glanced down once more at the typewritten list on her desk. It was then that she heard the gleeful, high-pitched laughter which rose to a shrill bubbling shriek—a shriek which pierced her eardrums even more painfully than the music had!

She rose to her feet, the bloodcurdling sound froze her to the spot. What was happening? Had Duval been taken ill? Was he having a fit of some kind?

Forgetting her fear, thinking that he might need help, she jerked the door open—and stood transfixed by the bizarre scene being enacted before her.

The lofty library was lit only by a single spotlight which blazed from a corner of the room; a tape recorder, its spools spinning, stood on the desk. Above it, a trapeze swung backward and forward like the pendulum of a clock. Facing it at the opposite end of the room, Pierre Duval swung on a second trapeze.

The stocky, dwarflike Frenchman wore only brief tights sparkling with rhinestones. On his round pink face was a grotesque grin, his mouth curled back over his teeth. He was laughing shrilly, and his eyes were bright with excitement as he swung back and forth, the muscles of his arms bulging, his body gleaming with sweat.

Then, with a shrill cry, he released his hold on the bar and sped through the air toward the trapeze swinging toward him, his arms and hands stretched straight before him. Ann caught her breath in a sudden gasp. If he misjudged the distance he would hurtle down to the stone floor below.

But she need not have worried. His strong hands closed around the metal bar, he swung up his legs with incredible agility, and sat astride the swinging trapeze, acknowledging the applause of some unseen audience.

There was happiness and excitement in his eyes, majesty in his bearing as he wiped his hands on a powdered cloth. He was in another world, a world of dreams, of ecstasy. Then he sensed he was not alone. His eyes became hooded, wary; the smile faded and was replaced by a frown.

He reached for a rope that dangled close to the now motionless trapeze and came down it hand over hand. On the floor he tossed the rope roughly aside and walked over to Ann. He looked angry.

"What are you doing here?" he demanded.

"I heard the music and . . . and . . ."

"You should know better than to enter the Big Top when an *artiste* is rehearsing," he said petulantly. His eyes still held the glassy stare she had observed earlier. It occurred to her at that moment that he might be under the influence of drugs.

"I'm sorry," she began, "but—"

"Sorry! So you should be. The public has no right in here! The evening performance does not start until eight—" He broke off rubbing his eyes. "Who are you? Your face is familiar. You speak English."

Ann touched his arm gently. "I'm your secretary, Ann Preston," she said. "Don't you remember?"

"What does an *artiste* like me want with a secretary?" he said, drawing himself up proudly. "I am Pierre Duval—the internationally famous trapeze *artiste!*"

Ann felt completely at a loss; this was a situation she could never have expected. She spoke soothingly: "I'm sure you are, M'sieu Duval. Your performance was superb."

His eyes lit up with pleasure. "You really think so?"

"I do," Ann nodded. "I mean it sincerely."

"It is very kind of you to say so," he murmured. "In that case, we will say nothing more about your trespassing here." Already he was slipping into the long dressing gown which had been draped over the back of a chair. "I will speak with the manager and have a complimentary ticket given to you . . ."

All at once his voice faltered. He passed a hand across his perspiring forehead, looked at her blankly, and then recognition flooded his eyes.

"Ann! Miss Preston!"

"Please sit down," she said gently. "I'll get you a glass of water."

"No, please—cognac. There's a bottle and glass in the bottom drawer of my desk."

A moment later he was sipping the drink and slowly the color came back into his cheeks. Sitting there in the swivel chair, swathed in the oversized dressing gown, he reminded Ann of a little boy who had misbehaved.

"I suppose you'll give in your notice now," he said regretfully.

She smiled. "Why should I?"

"You must have been very frightened—perhaps even amused at what you saw just now. It is only fair to tell you that I . . . I occasionally get these . . . attacks. . . ."

"Please don't worry on my behalf, M'sieu Duval. I can assure you I was not amused—only concerned in case you fell."

"I would not fall," he said. There was a distinct note of pride in his voice. "Until I took over the chateau from my brother, Juliette and I traveled the world with our act. That's where I met her—in the circus. She became part of the act," he smiled sadly, "although she doesn't like to be reminded of it now because an accident crippled her. She is a very good woman, but very proud of the name Duval and of this old house."

"She made you give up circus life?" Ann asked.

He nodded. "It was the sensible thing to do, I suppose. The estate is large, and the family has always had many business interests. But I loved the circus and my act. Perhaps it's because I'm forced to suppress my desire to continue in the circus that I have these attacks."

"It could be," Ann agreed. "But if they do you no harm . . ."

"They become less frequent as I grow older," he said. "Eventually they will cease altogether, I am told. When that day comes I think I shall be a very unhappy man." he sipped the brandy, shrugged his shoulders, and his round face creased again into a smile. "Of course, it is difficult to keep staff; they believe I may become violent and harm them. But they do not know me—I am *not* a violent man."

He offered her a cigarette and struck a match. Ann inhaled deeply, trying not to tell herself how incongruous the little scene was, Duval sitting there in his spangled tights, one trapeze still swinging slightly above them. She liked him—and these so-called fits did seem quite harmless; on the other hand she could well understand that his behavior was not likely to induce confidence in his servants.

"Have you seen a doctor—or a psychiatrist about them?" she asked. "The—attacks, I mean."

"Why should I?" His voice was suddenly harsh again. "There is nothing wrong with me! My act has always been an obsession with me! It must have its outlet! I injure no one! I am less harmless than Juliette's pet, am I not?"

"Pet?" Ann looked surprised; she had seen no animals about the chateau. "What kind of a pet? Has she a dog?"

He bit his lip. "You do not know about it? Then I shall be in trouble . . . I should not have mentioned it." He looked worried.

"But what is it?" repeated Ann, intrigued now.

"It is . . . a snake," he muttered. "Juliette keeps a python in a wicker basket—and when she is alone she talks to it. . . ."

And for the first time Ann thought she glimpsed an expression of fear upon his smooth cherubic face.

Chapter Seven

It was a long time before Ann slept that night. She had worked hard all evening, and yet the work had not seemed so very important—merely an inventory of the chateau's contents. The urgent job she had expected, which had necessitated her staying at the chateau, had not yet materialized.

Juliette and Yvette had spent the afternoon and evening shopping, which explained why neither of them had come to the library when Duval had his peculiar 'attack.' He had told Ann that these attacks were harmless, that he never became violent. But shouldn't he be in the care of a doctor, all the same?

And the snake, the python his wife apparently kept in the overheated lounge; the very thought of it made Ann's flesh creep. She hated snakes. That the Duvals were eccentric seemed to be an understatement, to say the least! And then there was the mysterious occupant of the west wing . . . the sooner she returned to Peggy's the better, she thought.

It was fine and sunny the following morning, and the sudden change in the weather helped to dispel some of her fears. Duval must have told Juliette of what had happened in the library, for the woman seemed worried at breakfast.

"I'm sorry you had such a distressing experience last night, Ann," she said, putting her cold, claw-like fingers on Ann's hand. Her dark eyes flickered over the girl's face anxiously.

"It did rather alarm me at first," Ann confessed.

"I do apologize. I suppose I should have warned you, but as you can understand, my husband's escapades—for want of a better word—are something of an embarrassment to us. We endeavor to keep them within the family. We had hoped that nothing like this would happen during your stay with us."

Yvette pushed back her plate with a gesture of distaste and lit a cigarette.

"If you ask me, it's the side effects of those tranquilizers he takes," she said. "That fool of a doctor . . . anyway, poor papa does no harm to anyone."

"Nevertheless," said her mother sharply, "it was not a pleasant experience for Miss Preston." She hesitated. "I do hope you will not decide to leave us because of it. We need you so much at this time."

Ann smiled reassuringly. "Please don't worry," she said. "I can assure you it makes no difference at all to me."

"So. That is good." Juliette was visibly relieved. "These attacks come very seldom now, sometimes only twice a month. I'm sure you will not be alarmed again."

"Don't let's talk about it any more," said Ann. She looked at her watch. "Please excuse me, I must start work now."

Ann got to her feet, folding her napkin and placing it in the silver napkin ring. But Juliette placed a detaining hand on her arm; her thin bloodless lips were parted in a smile.

"You have been very understanding, and I think that should bring its reward. Besides, you have been very industrious, working so late every evening. You do drive, yes?"

Ann nodded, wondering what was coming next.

"So. Then take the morning off. Go out and enjoy the fresh air."

Ann's face lit up. "That would be lovely! I do feel a little . . . stifled."

"Then you may leave as soon as you wish, my dear. I will arrange for the car to be placed at your disposal."

"Thank you. Thank you very much!" said Ann. Her eyes shining, she ran upstairs. The unexpectedness of the offer had pleased and surprised her. It meant that she would be able to see Steve after all.

Raymonde brought the car around as she descended the cracked steps leading to the front drive. "Madame instructed me to bring the car for you," he said solemnly.

Ann resisted a desire to giggle. With his gaunt unsmiling features and obsequious bow he was almost a caricature of an English stage butler, but she managed to keep a straight face.

"You will be careful, please, m'amselle? You will not stop for anything on the road? You may have heard that a girl was attacked—"

"I'll be careful," Ann promised. "And thank you."

It was fifteen miles to the village, and a pretty ride, for the road wound through picturesque green-wooded slopes and hamlets. Ann found herself looking forward to it, and she set out with a light heart. It was only half past eight, and she did not have to start work until two.

She wound the window down, and the breeze fanned her hair about her face as she depressed the accelerator. The sooner she reached the Continentale the sooner she would see Steve.

She roared down a road lined with trees, past fields where vines grew in orderly lines. Cafés with gaily colored umbrellas flashed past. She passed a heavy transporter rumbling toward the Spanish border. Now the road was winding down through wooded slopes, and the car was going along speedily.

She had to ease her foot down on the brake, but it did not respond. She exerted more pressure as a bend leapt toward her, and still nothing happened. She felt a swift upsurge of panic, as the wind whistled past the open window, cutting at her face.

She trod down hard on the brake. The car did not slow; on the contrary, it seemed to go even faster. The speedometer needle had crept up to sixty. The wind was now a roar in her ears, and the tires screamed as she hurtled around a second bend.

Thank God there was no traffic coming the other way!

The needle continued to creep up. Terror welled up inside her, filling her throat so that she could hardly breathe. Don't panic! screamed her mind. Don't panic, or you've had it!

Another bend leapt toward her. She double downshifted, snicked into second gear. The engine screamed. She was shot forward.

Another bend—a white fence coming toward her. The car lurched and skidded. She gripped the wheel tightly; the back began to swing around. She gritted her teeth, swung the wheel the other way. Tires screamed, shingle flew. The car slid across the road, then hit the fence. There was the harsh, tearing sound of metal biting into wood.

The car straightened, lurched across a narrow ditch, and tore its way through the tall leafy vines. The windshield had shattered, vines pushed inside. Then the car came to a grinding stop halfway up a bank . . . and began to roll backwards.

Her hands shaking, she grabbed the hand brake, heard it rasp on, and the car stopped moving. Then she sank back against the seat. She was drenched with perspiration, glistening globules trickled down her forehead, her cheeks were wet with it. She felt dizzy and closed her eyes.

The wave of nausea passed. After a few minutes Ann opened her eyes. She was still alive—and that was indeed something to be grateful for. A stifled sob broke from her throat. Her fingers quivered as she groped wildly for her cigarettes, her lighter. She dropped it and as she bent to retrieve it, the world spun around again.

She grabbed at the lighter, thumbed it, sucked smoke deeply into her lungs. "Oh God, thank you," she whispered. Then there came a thunderous roaring in her ears, and she felt herself plunging down and down into a deep, bottomless pit. . . .

When she recovered consciousness there was something soft beneath her head. Pain stabbed behind her eyes and there was a sour, acid taste in her mouth. She moaned as she opened her eyes.

"Relax, m'amselle."

She found herself gazing into the friendly features of a deeply tanned gendarme with a thin black mustache and a cap worn at a jaunty angle. She sat up to find that she had been lying on the grassy bank; his jacket had been beneath her head for a pillow. His motorcycle was parked on the side of the road.

"You are feeling better?" he asked solicitously.

"Thank you, yes."

"The ambulance will not be long." He smiled.

"But I don't need an ambulance. I'm all right." She began to protest. "I'm not even hurt, just bruised."

"Perhaps, yes. But you will need something to take you back to the chateau."

Ann looked at him startled. "How did you know I came from the chateau?"

"I needed some means of identification," he explained. "There was a letter in your bag." He appraised her thoughtfully. "Did you have any friends with you?"

She stared at him in surprise; he was not smiling now. "No. I was traveling alone."

"Perhaps you were going too fast because you were being chased?"

"Of course not!" She shook her head in bewilderment. "The brakes failed coming down the hill. What makes you think I was being chased?"

He removed his cap and wiped his forehead with his handkerchief. The sun was shining down out of a cloudless blue sky. It was very warm. It started out to be a lovely day, Ann thought dismally, and here I am waiting for an ambulance and answering stupid questions. Did he think she had been having a race with some friends?

"M'amselle," he said slowly, "when I stopped I saw two men. They were parked in a car at the side of the road. They got out and began to walk toward your car, but when they saw me they turned back and drove off. Do you know anything about that?"

She shook her head. "Somebody passing who had stopped to help I suppose. When they saw you arrive they decided they didn't have to get involved."

"They were nothing to do with you? You weren't having a race?"

"I wouldn't do anything so stupid!" she said. "I've just told you! I was coming down the hill and the brakes failed."

"Very well. I accept your word." He gave a stiff little bow. "I think I should trace these people. I have seen them before; they are Americans."

Ann gave a start. "Had one of them a beard?"

"But yes. Then you do know them?"

"No, but I had been told they were in the village."

"I see."

First they had been hanging about the chateau, thought Ann; now they had not been far behind her when she had crashed. Coincidence? Surely it *must* be. Why should two Americans be interested in her?

The thought left her mind when the ambulance drew up, and a doctor alighted from it. He insisted upon examining her. "You have been born under a lucky star," he said a little later. "But there might be delayed shock. I think it would be advisable for you to stay at the hospital for the night."

"But I feel perfectly all right!" she protested. "Besides, I have someone to meet in the village. Please drop me off there."

The doctor straightened and sat down on the stretcher, facing her. He was making notes on a pad.

"I'm sorry," he said. "It is not possible. It would mean traveling in the opposite direction. I cannot insist that you go to the hospital—but we shall be passing the chateau."

She sighed and resigned herself to disappointment. She had wanted so much to see Steve. But certainly she did not feel up to walking the rest of the way to the village. There was nothing to do but to accept the offer of a lift and return to the chateau.

She frowned as she thought of the car in which she had set out so lightheartedly. Why had the brakes failed like that? It was a comparatively new car, as far as she could see. And, in any case, surely it was regularly checked?

"We must leave now, m'amselle," the doctor said. "You wish to be taken home?"

She nodded listlessly.

A few moments later she was inside the ambulance, and it was moving quickly away from the scene. There was a newspaper lying on the seat inside, so she picked it up, not out of curiosity but in an attempt to divert her mind from her near-accident and her uncomfortable thoughts about the events before and after it.

It was the early edition of the local newspaper, published only that morning. The black banner headline was splashed across the front page:

GIRL ATTACKED
Admitted to Hospital Suffering from Shock

But it was not this which held Ann's horrified gaze; inset beside the story was a photograph of the girl. She looked at it, and felt as though another nightmare were just about to begin.

The girl in the photograph looked almost like the girl whose picture she had seen in the room of the deserted west wing!

Chapter Eight

Juliette Duval was deeply shocked when Ann arrived back at the chateau in an ambulance. Her shawl clutched about her narrow shoulders, she tapped her way across the cavern-like hall.

"*Mon Dieu!* What has happened? I saw the ambulance outside—"

"There was an accident with the car—" Ann began.

The Frenchwoman's eyes probed hers. "You have not been hurt?"

"No, just shaken up."

"So. That is a great relief. But you are pale. You need a drink. Come, you can tell me about it."

She took Ann into the lounge on the second floor, where a fire glowed in the old-fashioned fireplace. The room was like an oven. Ann felt her skin creep as what she knew must be the snake moved restlessly inside a wicker basket on the floor.

Juliette listened in silence as Ann related what had happened. "That is terrible!" she exclaimed when the girl had finished. "That the brakes should have failed at such a time! You might have been killed! I would never have forgiven myself if anything had happened to you. Pierre will be most upset when he hears . . . he will have a few words to say to Yvette when she comes in."

"It's Yvette's car, then?"

"But yes. The stupid girl! She is the wild one. She should see that it is properly serviced. Now, if only my son Gaston were alive . . . he could do anything with cars . . . such a clever boy, even though I say it myself." She smiled apologetically. "Mothers always think the world of their sons; they can do no wrong."

Ann shifted uncomfortably. "Yvette is not yet out of her teens," she murmured, trying to excuse the girl. "Young people are often thoughtless—and reckless too. But one day I expect she will settle down and get married."

"Perhaps." Juliette drew herself up proudly. "But it must be someone who will be worthy of becoming a member of our family. She must not marry just anyone!"

Ann smiled and said, "Is she in the garden? Somebody will have to see about getting the car back. And of course I must explain to her what happened."

"She has gone out. Did I not say? The young American called for her."

Ann's heart gave a little lurch. "American?"

"But yes. It is someone she met in the village a few days ago. He rang up yesterday."

Ann's mouth tightened. So that was it? Steve had telephoned Yvette and had received an invitation to the chateau. He had obviously hoped to see Ann, but Yvette had made sure that she was out. No doubt it had been Yvette who had suggested to her mother that Ann should be given the morning off. So even if she had gone to the village she would have missed him.

She got to her feet, put down her empty glass. Juliette appeared to have forgotten her existence because the woman was leaning forward, patting the wicker basket and crooning softly. The basket was creaking, and Ann felt a mixture of horror and revulsion sweep over her. She must get out of this horribly oppressive room before she fainted.

"I think I had better start work," Ann managed to say.

"As you wish." Juliette spoke absently. "But don't overdo things. If I were you I would make it a short session."

Ann went downstairs to her office, although she did not feel very much like work. She had so looked forward to her morning off and to seeing Steve that now the reaction had set in she felt terribly depressed and uneasy. But the fact that Yvette was with Steve was not the sole reason for her mood; she was puzzled by the interest which the bearded American appeared to be taking in her.

Then there was the matter of the photograph of the girl in the newspaper; it seemed incredible that she should be the twin of the one in the room in the west wing. And, as for the west wing, what about its mysterious occupant?

She wondered if she should inform the police. A hundred and one questions chased through her mind, but she could not provide sensible or convincing answers to any of them. Puzzling over them brought on a splitting headache, and presently she took a couple of aspirins and went upstairs to her room to lie down on the bed.

She must have dozed, for when she next glanced around the room it was in total darkness. For a moment she lay there, then she sat up, gazing at the luminous dial of her watch—seven o'clock!

Heavens, no wonder she felt hungry! She had slept practically the whole afternoon. Still, she supposed it had been kind of them not to disturb her.

She decided to go downstairs and make herself a sandwich. Swinging off the bed, she crossed to the window to draw the curtains. It was a bright, starlit night and the grounds and the lake beyond were bathed in the pale yellow light of the moon. The twisted misshapen trees surrounding the water were sharply etched against the sky.

She was reaching up for the curtains when she froze. Two people had just emerged from a small copse close to the house. They were talking earnestly together, but there was no mistaking them.

It was Raymonde, the butler—and Steve!

Lew Vorrelli removed his black-rimmed sunglasses and stared with watery, protuberant eyes at the man known as Max.

The thin, pallid-faced American was hunched over a table in the window of the small villa they had rented near the coast. A square of white cardboard was in front of him, and on it was a half completed watercolor painting of the view from the window: the garden in the foreground, bright with flowers, the sand dunes beyond, the puffs of white clouds over the sea.

Max had always been a source of constant surprise to Vorrelli. This time Max's talent for painting in watercolors fascinated the man. Max might be dumb in more ways than one, and girl crazy, but he was a master with a paintbrush. The color work was bold, vivid, violent, like the man himself. It was good, very good.

"You have real talent, Max," he siad.

"Think so?"

"I know so."

"What makes you think you know?" Max asked sourly.

"I collect paintings. I have a friend, an art dealer; he's taught me a lot. You've painted much lately?"

"No—as a kid, yes. It was something to do. It made you forget the hunger in your guts. It got me out of the dump where me and the old lady and eight other kids lived. Some old fool at school used to encourage me." He grinned. "He didn't know that all I wanted was peace and quiet, free coffee, and something to eat."

Vorrelli smiled. "No wonder you got an eye for the dollies. It's the artist in you."

"Yeah," said Max and he belched.

He put down the paintbrush, tired of the painting. It had been something to do while Vorrelli was out. He watched as the plump, bearded man filled two glasses with cognac.

"How did you make out?"

"Okay. Miguel's catching the next flight out. He'll be here tomorrow. We're going to need him."

"I thought you said you was going to take a look at the chateau."

"I did." Vorrelli passed one of the glasses. "Drink that, and we'll be on our way."

"You're in a hurry."

"Sure I am. I don't want that French cop nosing around and asking too many questions."

Max's thin features twisted. "That was bad luck if anything was. We'd have got the girl if he hadn't showed up." He rubbed his nose. "She must be one of those hard-working dolls. Never goes out, works and sleeps there."

"That's just it," grunted Vorrelli.

"Huh?"

"Because they don't want her out of their sight. Remember, they got reasons too, like we have. I've a hunch they tried to kill her."

"What makes you think so?"

Vorrelli said: "I been making discreet enquiries in the village. Know what?"

"You tell me."

"Someone had been tampering with the car brakes. That's why she crashed."

Max's eyes widened. He whistled softly through his teeth. "I get the message. We gotta talk to her before she gets herself killed."

"That's why I've been up at the chateau. There's an old wing—it's a tumbledown joint so the rooms have been closed, it's not lived in any more. Well, I've found a way in. It shouldn't be too difficult for a guy with your talents."

Max's wolfish face creased in a grin. "Okay. I've been waiting for some action. Let's go."

"That's the way in," Vorrelli said, later that evening, as they crouched in the bushes at the foot of the old chateau wall. "I've been part of the way. It leads to the cellars. There's a passage that goes right beneath the building. The chic works on the ground floor. You got the map I drew?"

"Sure." Max patted his pocket.

"And make it quick. I don't want to hang around here too long. Someone might spot the car."

"Half hour; that's all I need."

Max dragged the bushes to one side and disappeared through a hole in the castle wall. It was pitch dark inside, and he groped for his pocket-torch. He directed the powerful light about the cellar, getting his bearings. He had a good memory for detail. The map Vorrelli had drawn was deeply etched in his mind.

A lot of old junk, he thought, as he stared around him. Old tables, furniture, rusty springs protruding through the chair seats, broken benches, crates, shelving . . . rubble everywhere.

He moved silently through a doorway that led to the cellar beyond. There were, he discovered, five cellars in all beneath the old wing. Large places, four and five times as big as the room where he had been brought up—and these were just the cellars!

It was a funny world, he reflected. Some folk

had it all; a smart house, a beautiful doll, and bread in the bank. Others like his ma had eight noisy kids, a smelly overcrowded dump, a toilet that you shared with a dozen other families, and an old man who boozed his time away in pool rooms.

He crept forward, shining the torch beam before him. Ahead he could see a pool of water and beyond that the entrance to the passage that Vorrelli had told him about.

Not far to go now, and it should be easy enough to get the girl. The Duvals relaxed after the evening meal; she would be on her own.

Then he stopped dead in his tracks, sniffing. What gave? It had been stinking here a few minutes ago; like a sewer. Now there was another kind of smell—like a downtown brothel. Reminded him of a babe he'd met in Paris. That dolly had been all curves and softness and—

Then it happened.

Fingers like vices closed about his throat from behind. He cried out, struggled, but there was no escape. The hands were like steel clamps.

He knew then, quite suddenly, that this was it. He was going to die, and there was nothing he could do about it.

Chapter Nine

Ann saw Steve and Raymonde disappear from view; it looked as though they were coming toward the chateau, but she did not hesitate. Steve, she thought, must be enquiring about her. Then she frowned. No, that couldn't be it. He would have come up to the house.

Oh, what did it matter? She must see him.

She snatched up her flashlight to see her way along the dark corridor and down the stairs. The big, cavernous hall was empty, and the house silent as a tomb. She saw that a small door leading to the cellars was open, but that was no concern of hers. Perhaps Marie was still on duty and had gone down to the wine cellar.

She would have passed it without giving it a second glance, but suddenly there came a faint cry from the darkness below. She stopped, breathing hard, straining her ears. She must have been mistaken—there was nothing. She started forward again, and almost immediately the wavering cry was repeated.

A man's voice, hoarse and frightened. *Steve?* Could it be Steve, in danger! Had Raymonde tricked him into the cellars for some sinister motive of his own?

Her heart racing, Ann stepped inside. A flight of wooden steps led downward. Cautiously she descended them and found herself in a large cellar. There were piles of broken furniture, a heavy old sideboard with cracked mirrors, its doors missing. Next to it were rickety chairs, a broken table and some crates filled with empty bottles.

Beyond them were wooden shelves. They leaned at a crazy angle against the cellar wall. Broken bottles were scattered about the floor, reminding her of a fight scene she had seen on television.

She would have crept on but in the circle of light she saw a dark opening behind the shelves. She drew closer, and crouched to see that it was the entrance to a small or dark passage. Finding it did not surprise her. The chateau was hundreds of years old, was probably honeycombed with secret passages. Some of these old chateaux were as steeped in history—and violence—as any manor house or castle in Britain.

She listened. She could hear no sound, but the cry for help must have come from here. The passage was just over shoulder width, and at times she had to walk sideways. It was cold and damp, and here and there repulsive-looking fungi sprouted from the walls.

The passage began to wind down into the very bowels of the earth, it seemed. At a rough guess she judged it was somewhere beneath the west wing, for in places the brick foundations were revealed. Presently it began to widen into a large cellar. There was a pile of rubble in one corner where a flight of stone steps had once stood. Water had dribbled down at some time and formed a large, evil-smelling pool.

Her heart thudding, Ann realized that there was no one in the cellar. Nevertheless, her nerves were still stretched taut as she again advanced. Now she had the feeling that she was not alone, that hidden eyes were watching her.

She reached the pool, then recoiled with a cry of horror. The figure of a man was sprawled face-down in the water, his arms stretched out stiffly before him. He was partially submerged.

She saw that he was dark haired, and wore a dark gray suit with a pinstripe. Scum was forming around the thick gold band on the small finger of his right hand. She turned away shivering.

It was no good; she couldn't stay here a moment longer. It must have been this man, this stranger, who had cried for help, not Steve. And he was obviously beyond all help now.

Then another thought struck her, almost rooting her to the ground with terror: The murderer could still be down here!

She stumbled back along the narrow, winding passage. It seemed an age before she finally reached the stone steps in the cellar and hurried up them into the hall. As always, the vast room was still and silent.

She almost ran across it and into her office.

"Is that you, Ann?" For the first time she realized that the communicating door was ajar. It opened and Duval stood there, puffing at his pipe. He padded forward, his round, childlike face was concerned.

"Is anything the matter? You are very pale." He called over his shoulder, "Juliette!"

Ann said, "There's a—dead man down in the cellar!"

"What?" Duval gaped at her, his mouth wide.

Juliette limped into the room. Her thin yellow face was set, and her eyes glinted.

"A dead man?" She spoke sharply.

"In a pool beneath the west wing," said Ann.

The Frenchwoman's mouth tightened. "I thought I made it quite clear to you that you were not to—"

"I know," said Ann. "But I was passing when I thought I heard a cry. I thought perhaps you or M'sieu Duval had met with an accident."

"Go on."

"I went down into the cellar. I found an old passage . . ." For a moment Ann thought she saw indecision and alarm flicker across Juliette's face, then it was gone. Juliette turned and spoke briskly to her husband.

"Well, don't stand there like an imbecile! Get a torch!"

"Yes, yes, I have one in my desk," he said hurriedly. "Shall I call Raymonde, my dear?"

"Of course not," she said testily. "We've lost enough staff; we don't want to lose him as well. It's dark down there. Ann probably imagined it all."

Ann flushed and said angrily, "I can assure you I did nothing of the kind!"

The Frenchwoman's thin lips compressed. "Very well, we shall see. Come along."

Ann said, "It's in a cellar at the end of the passage. You may find it difficult to gett here."

"Nothing is impossible to me," said Juliette firmly. "You will lead the way with the torch, Pierre—" Her eyes narrowed as she looked at Ann. "I know of this passage; it used to lead to the wine cellars in the old wing. But I haven't been there for many years."

"What puzzles me is how the man got in there in the first place," Duval muttered.

"It wouldn't be difficult," said his wife. "The

walls are crumbling away, as you know. In future we must see that the passage is blocked."

"But what would he be doing there?" persisted Duval.

"Who knows? Perhaps it was a tramp."

"He wasn't dressed like one," said Ann quickly.

"Then perhaps he was a thief, hoping to get into the chateau. He didn't realize, of course, that there was danger—and got more than he bargained for!"

Was that the answer, Ann wondered, as they stumbled along the passage. But who had killed him, the mysterious occupant of the west wing?

At last they emerged into the last cellar. Duval directed the torch beam about the damp walls, finally bringing the circle of light to the pool.

"This body . . . I don't see it!" Juliette spoke impatiently.

"It's in the pool," said Ann, with a little shiver as she stepped forward. Then her eyes widened incredulously.

The pool was empty. The body had vanished!

"Well, Ann?" There was an edge to Juliette's voice as she turned, leaning heavily on her walking stick. Ann could have sworn there was a glint of triumph in the dark eyes. Bathed in that circle of torch light, her face seemed more yellow, the lines more deeply etched, the bloodless lips thinner. She looked older, witchlike stooped in the black shawl draped around her shoulders.

"But I . . . don't understand." Ann stammered. "It was here! I saw it! I can describe his clothes." She stared blankly at the dark stagnant pool. Not a ripple stirred the surface.

"*I* understand very well." Juliette's voice was acid. "You imagined it all. Shadows."

"But she distinctly said—" began Duval.

"She was mistaken!" Juliette's voice rasped. "Shadows cast by the torch, overwrought nerves, too much imagination. Let us go back. I can feel the damp penetrating my bones."

"Very well, my dear," he said meekly.

Ann's head was in a whirl as she took one last glance at the silent pool, then turned to follow them. She knew she had not imagined it, whatever the woman might say. It had not been a trick of light or shadow. The color of the man's hair, the gray pin-striped suit he was wearing, the gold band on his finger—all were still vividly in her mind's eye. She knew she would never forget the sight as long as she lived.

Obviously, she thought, somebody had removed the corpse—Somebody who did not want the police wandering about the old building, perhaps identifying the dead man.

The Duvals? Raymonde, the butler?

It couldn't be anyone else. But if it were Raymonde, was Steve involved?

No, she couldn't believe he was mixed up in murder. That left only the Duvals. What were they up to in this gloomy old chateau? What had the dead man seen—or known—that he had to have been silenced?

Marie, the maid, appeared in the hall. She brushed down her crisp linen apron. "Monsieur Langognes has been telephoning, m'amselle Preston," she said.

"Thank you, Marie."

As the girl disappeared in the direction of the servants' quarters, Juliette touched Ann's arm.

"Please, if you telephone him—you will say nothing about this. There is enough talk about us already, without adding to it." Then, as Ann hesitated: "Please—I beg of you!"

"Very well," said Ann turning away.

"I am going upstairs, Pierre," Juliette said abruptly, and limped up the stairs and into the lounge.

The curtains in the lounge had been drawn back and Yvette was lounging in one of the fireside chairs, smoking a cigarette.

"Must you draw back the curtains when you know how it irritates me!" Juliette spoke venomously. At the sound of her voice the python in the wicker basket stirred restlessly. "There, there," she went on softly, her voice changing on the instant. "I didn't mean to disturb you. Go back to sleep. Put some more coal on the fire, Yvette. He mustn't catch cold."

Yvette shivered, despite the fact that the room was like a furnace. "*Must* you keep that horrible thing?"

"We have always been together."

"It gives me the creeps!"

"He gives me a great deal more comfort than you do," said Juliette crossly. "Where have you been?"

"Out."

"With that American—Steve Martin?"

"I have." Yvette spoke defiantly.

Her mother gave her a shrewd glance. "You're in love with him?"

"I could be. I don't know."

"What *do* you know about him?"

Yvette stared sullenly. "He's a writer. I've already told you that. He's doing research on a book about chateaux, and I'm helping him."

"Has he told you anything about himself?"

"He's widely traveled—that's obvious—and he lived for a while in Copenhagen."

"Has he mentioned his background, his family?"

The girl flared. "What is this—an inquisition?

Are you so afraid you'll have an undesirable in the family? That's a laugh!"

"Don't talk to me like that!" Juliette said harshly. "I have good reason for asking these questions. It has nothing to do with pride. Now, tell me, what do you know about his family?"

"His father is a wealthy stockbroker," the girl answered sulkily. "His mother died two years ago. He visits his father once or twice a year in Washington."

"I see. Juliette lit a cigarette. This was unusual, so her daughter stared at her, surprised, since Juliette strongly disapproved of smoking. Something was most definitely wrong.

"What's the matter? Why all these questions about Steve?" Yvette uncoiled herself and got languidly to her feet. She was wearing bright yellow slacks, her figure swelling against the purple nylon blouse.

"Your father has been worried about two Americans who have been hanging about the chateau," said Juliette. "And so am I."

"You see danger everywhere," the girl said impatiently, flicking her silken black hair away from her eyes. "Your generation always does!"

"Perhaps not without good reason," her mother retorted. "It's possible this man Steven is friendly with them. They could be old friends of your uncle's and—"

"That I can't believe!" Yvette cut in.

"He could be using you in order to get into the chateau and look around."

"I'm a good judge of character," Yvette said curtly. "I tell you, there's nothing to be suspicious about where Steve is concerned."

Juliette bit her lip. "Has he ever mentioned your Uncle Henri?"

"No."

"And have you?"

"Of course not."

"Well, don't!"

"Look, what's all this about?" Yvette's voice was suddenly sharp with anger.

"I've told you: some Americans seem to be showing an interest in the chateau. In fact, I believe one of them has been killed in the cellar, trying to get in."

Yvette went white. "You don't mean that—"

"He was taken care of. But it was Ann who found him."

"That means we'll have the police crawling about the place!"

Juliette shook her head. "By the time we got down there, the body had been removed."

At this Yvette smiled ironically. "What did Ann say to that?"

"Naturally she was startled. I think I managed

to convince her that she had imagined it, that it had been a trick of the light."

"She's no fool," said Yvette.

"I agree. That's why another attempt must be made to get rid of her."

Yvette shivered suddenly beneath the cold malignant expression in her mother's eyes. "I don't like her. Steve's too fond of her for my liking," she admitted. "But murder—"

"There's no other way," Juliette said calmly.

"You must be mad. Anyway, I don't want to know. If it weren't for Steve I'd have gone back to Paris long ago. Maybe I will soon."

"You'll go when I say. That place isn't good for you."

The girl sneered. "I'll go when I feel like it, not when *you* say so!"

She stubbed out her cigarette and stalked out, her eyes bright with defiance. She hated the chateau; it stifled her. Besides, in many ways her parents frightened her. There was her father, living in the past, having these extraordinary and terrifying bouts of madness. But of the two, it was her mother of whom she was most afraid. Juliette was obsessed with one idea. She was sick. She and that slimy thing in the basket!

Yvette felt tired and bitter as she wandered into the hall. The stoop-shouldered Raymonde was just replacing the telephone receiver. He stared at her with his cold, almost antagonistic eyes.

"You are going out, m'amselle?"

"Only for a walk on the grounds."

"Please—do not go far," he said quietly. "A girl has been attacked in the village and there have been strange men hanging around the chateau."

"Oh, don't you start. I shall be all right." She gave an almost savage laugh. "I don't think *I'm* likely to be attacked." She wandered out onto the patio.

The morning had not proved to be the enjoyable one she had expected. Earlier she had flung her bikini and a towel into the back of the estate car and driven into the village. She had found Steve in the bar on the Continentale and not for the first time was impressed by how attractive he was, tall and dark, with laughing eyes, and a firm mouth. He wore green slacks and a gaily colored shirt with a red and blue tie.

He looked surprised. "I wasn't expecting you this morning!"

"I was on my way to the coast, and I thought I'd look in."

He nodded absently. It had been a disappointment not seeing Ann at the chateau, and he'd been alarmed when he'd learned later that she had been involved in an accident. Yvette had told him that she was in bed and that there was nothing to worry about, but he was still concerned.

"What will you have?" he said.

"I don't think I want a drink right now, Steve." She flashed him a smile and moved closer so that her perfume wafted to his nostrils. "There's a ruined chateau about five miles from here, right on the coast. It's almost tumbling into the sea. This time next year it will probably have been washed away."

"Well?"

"It would make an item of unusual interest," she went on quickly. "You must include a photograph, and while we're there I will tell you its history." She smiled up at him provocatively. "I promise, you will find the trip most rewarding."

Steve hesitated—and was lost. She hooked her arm through his and pulled him towards the door.

"Come on," she said gaily. "No slacking! You have to work, you know, not prop up bars."

"I guess you're right," he admitted reluctantly.

"Of course I'm right! The evening is for fun—and I mean to see that you keep at your work during the day."

She was an intelligent conversationalist, and he had to admit that she was good company.

"I was surprised to learn that Ann Preston had moved into the chateau," he said. "Your father must be keeping her very busy."

"I wouldn't know. I have nothing to do with the running of the business."

"Then you don't know how long she'll be at the chateau?"

"Not really," she replied disinterestedly.

She swung left on the coast road. Here there were sand dunes and scattered pink-washed villas with wooden steps leading down to the beach. At last she turned off the road, drove for fifty yards down a sandy track and then braked.

"This is it," she said happily. "It's one of my favorite spots. I come here to think sometimes. You're very privileged."

He grinned. "Thanks. I appreciate it."

"Let's get out. Bring the camera; you'll get a better shot from the beach, with the rocks in close foreground."

"You know something about angles and shots?" he asked surprised.

"Not really—but I've done some modeling in Paris. They're always talking technical. But don't tell mama; she'd have a fit! A Duval modeling! *Mon Dieu!*" She threw up her hands in mock horror. "Terrible! And without clothes!"

He grinned. He had known her long enough to realize that she was a strange girl, gay, provocative, an infectious laugh one minute, moody and sullen the next if she could not have her own way. A difficult girl, a child even, still immature, fiery and rebellious, possessive, and probably half the time unable to explain her actions even to herself.

"It's certainly visual," he said raising the camera.

As she had said, the remains of the old chateau were balanced precariously on the rocks, overlooking the quiet, peaceful bay. Only one red brick spire and part of the wall remained. It had been buffeted and beaten by the winds of centuries, and most of it had disappeared into the sea. There was rubble and bricks amongst the rocks below it, and the sea washed in and out, leaving a soapy, lather-like foam behind, tiny pools in the wet sand.

"And am I?" she asked.

"Are you what?"

"Visual?"

She was a picture of loveliness standing there, her eyes mocking, her shapely lips parted to reveal perfect teeth. She looked very desirable.

"You don't have to ask me that," he said.

"Then tell me," she pouted. "*Am* I visual?"

"Very."

"And so are you, Steve."

Her heady perfume assailed him. She was very close. Then her arms went up about his neck, and her fingers tightened; her lips fastened hungrily upon his mouth.

For a moment he responded to the warmth of her kiss, then he gently disengaged her arms from around his neck. "I think we'd better be getting back," he said gently.

She went rigid. Her face was flushed, and just for a moment she looked almost ugly.

"What's the matter, Steve?" she flashed at him.

"Nothing," he said. "It's just that . . . well, I think we ought to get back." He forced a laugh. "Besides, you haven't told me anything about this old ruin."

"To hell with it!" she said. "What's wrong with *me?*"

"Nothing's wrong, Yvette. But it's time to go. I'm expecting a telephone call at one o'clock."

"Forget it. Let's stay here." Her voice came softly, caressingly, and her arms began to entwine about his neck once more. But he stopped her.

"It's important," he said.

"Liar!"

"You shouldn't say that, I—"

"You're lying," she said, her voice rising shrilly. "You're not expecting any call. It's just an excuse. It's just that you don't want me." Her face was flushed, and her breast was heaving against the tight blouse.

He said quietly: "You're very desirable, Yvette. I know it—and you know it . . . but you're just not for me."

"It's that girl, Ann, isn't it? You're in love with *her?*"

Steve frowned, then nodded. "Okay, if you want the truth. Yes, I'm in love with Ann."

"But she's not your kind!" Words spilled quickly from her lips. "*I'm* your kind, Steve! I could make you happy! We could have such fun! I know it. We could live together!"

"You're wrong, Yvette. Ann is very much my type of girl."

"And I'm not?"

"I didn't say that," he said helplessly.

"But you meant it!"

"I did not." He spoke sharply, then glanced anxiously at his wristwatch. "And it was true about that telephone call. I must get back."

"Damn you! Damn the telephone call! Damn Ann Preston! You'll not get her!" She was becoming hysterical. Sobbing, she turned suddenly and ran back to the car. Almost in the same instant he realized her intention. He ran forward, but she was already behind the steering wheel. She revved, the engine roared, and the car hurtled backward recklessly.

"Yvette! Stop!"

He thought he heard her laugh, shrilly, mockingly. She shouted something, but it was borne away on the breeze. He ran, but the car was already out of sight amongst the sand dunes. By the time he reached the coast road there was no sign of it.

She had left him there, furious and fuming. . . .

No, she reflected now, as she wandered disconsolately in the overgrown gardens of the chateau, it wasn't a very happy morning.

She'd always been quick tempered, hasty and impulsive. Now she'd made things worse. She should have retained her self-control; there was more than one way of getting a man. She should have played it cool, not gone off the deep end the way she had done. What a fool she had been, to be sure! Never mind, though, she still had a chance.

Ann wouldn't be here much longer, would she?

But the thought sent a cold shiver down her spine. She turned suddenly and ran back to the chateau.

Chapter Ten

Ann took a break from typing and lit a cigarette. Outside she could hear Juliette sharply telling her husband to waste no time in bricking up the entrance to the passage Ann had found the previous day. Plainly the woman was worried; there was no question of that. But: Did she want the passage closed because the body was still down there, and she wanted to conceal it? Or was she merely safeguarding the treasures in the chateau?

Ann stared at the afternoon sunshine glistening on the lake and wondered what she should do. Ever since she had found the body in the pool she had been very uneasy and frightened. There was so much that was inexplicable.

What was the strange scent that always accompanied the sensation she had of being watched? Had the dead man been the mysterious occupant of the west wing? Then there was the girl who had been attacked—the girl who so closely resembled the photograph Ann had found in the hidden room. Were they one and the same?

The more she thought about it the more convinced she was that something terrifying was taking place in the old chateau, with its rattling doors and windows, its shadowy passages, and even more shadowy corners.

The sensible thing, she thought, would be to give in her notice, to leave at once. There was nothing to hold her here; she was under no obligation to stay. They would want an explanation, of course . . . well, she would tell them the truth, that the old house and working on her own was too much for her. Once away from it all she could get everything in its true perspective, tell Steve and seek his advice.

A quiet tap on the door interrupted her thoughts. Raymonde came in carrying her afternoon coffee and a plate of biscuits.

"Where's Marie?" asked Ann surprised.

"She's left, m'amselle—it's her short day."

"Oh, I see. Thank you." He did not leave immediately and, glancing up, she saw his cold gaze on her. "Is anything wrong?" she asked.

"No. I was just thinking that you looked rather white when you came up from the cellar yesterday. Was anything wrong?"

Not unless you can call finding a dead body wrong, thought Ann. Aloud she said, "No."

"I have not known the family to visit the cellars for many months." His brow was furrowed in a frown. Was he pumping her? wondered Ann.

"It was nothing," she said. "I thought I heard someone cry out, but I must have been mistaken."

He bowed his head and then smiled. It was the first time she had seen him smile since she had been at the chateau, and she was agreeably surprised to find that his smile was kind and gentle.

"I hope you will not forget what I said the other night, m'amselle. If you need my help at any time, please let me know. This house—and sometimes its owners—can be, how shall I put it, strange? I shall always be pleased to advise and help." Then he went out, closing the door behind him.

Ann was suspicious. Had he been sent by the Duvals to test her, to see what she would say about seeing the body in the pool? If so, it had been rather a clumsy attempt.

If only she could see Steve and talk over everything with him! She remembered his meeting with Raymonde; perhaps Steve had asked the butler to keep an eye on her. That could be a natural explanation as to why they had been together. If he couldn't be at the chateau himself.

Her spirits lifted a little, and she picked up the telephone, asking the operator to put her through to Peggy. She had spoken to Tom the previous night before going up to bed and had promised to call him again.

Peggy sounded very pleased to hear from her.

"Tom's been worrying ever since you telephoned last night. He thought you sounded—well, as though you were under some kind of strain."

"I was just tired, but it's sweet of him to worry. Is he there?"

"The poor lamb's had to go to Rouen. And I have to fly to Paris tonight. But are you really all right, dear?"

"Of course I am." She couldn't unload her troubles on them now, particularly not from the chateau. Somebody could be listening on the extension; she wouldn't put it past them.

"You're quite sure?" Peggy persisted. "Oh, it worries me your working up there. I wish you'd give notice and come home. I shall be back on Thursday, and perhaps we'll talk it over, eh? I'm sure you could soon get another job, and I'd feel so much happier." She babbled on, a sure sign that something was troubling her: "You know, Ann, I've an awful feeling that something is going to happen. They still haven't caught the beast who attacked that poor girl."

Ann said, "It *is* rather lonely, working here on my own. I may do as you say, Peggy, and look for something else. We'll talk about it when you come back."

She hung up then and spent the remainder of the afternoon typing some urgent returns for Duval's partner in Paris. But she felt unusually tired, and when it was time for dinner she leaned back in her chair with a sigh of relief.

Yvette had spent the afternoon crying on her bed. Emotionally exhausted, she had fallen asleep. Gray shadows were filling the bedroom when she awoke, feeling heavy and sticky-eyed. She sipped a glass of water poured from the carafe on her bedside table, then lit a cigarette.

She had cried herself to sleep, but now her mood had changed; her expression was hard and bitter. All her life she had been used to having her own way; her father had gratified her every wish. The fact that she had been unable to get what she wanted from Steve was a new and humiliating experience. She felt chagrined as well as angry.

This was the first time a man had not responded ardently to her kisses. She felt spurned, frustrated, embittered. And it did not help to remember that she had been rebuffed because of an innocent English girl with large eyes and long spindly legs. Surely with Ann out of the way Steve could not possibly resist her for long, she thought, glancing at herself in the long mirror.

But this time she must play it cautiously. She must show concern for Ann, be sympathetic and understanding. If she used the right tactics he would, in the end, turn to her for comfort.

She glanced up irritably as her mother came into the room.

Juliette looked frail and tired. It was almost unbelievable that a woman could age so much in the space of a few years. There were heavy shadows beneath her eyes, lines deeply drawn in what had once been a pretty face, and the thin lips were almost colorless. Oh yes, she had made it all too clear who had been her favorite child.

Gaston! It had always been Gaston. Gaston this, Gaston that, ever since Yvette had been an elfin-faced child with braids.

Why can't you be like Gaston? The dear boy— he's always so thoughtful. Now why couldn't you have brought me flowers on my wedding anniversary? Gaston never forgets anything.

Gaston! *Always* Gaston! In fact, sometimes Yvette wondered if Juliette had forgotten her completely, forgotten that she even existed. It was never: *Oh, doesn't that dress suit you. You're so pretty! That's very sweet of you, darling! Enjoy yourself, dear.*

Not a kindly glance, a caress, or even a friendly smile for Yvette. Only for Gaston.

Juliette had aged—but Yvette could feel no compassion for her, no sympathy. She liked papa because they were two of a kind: the unloved; the forgotten. And, of course, they had much in common. Her father too had been wild in his youth. As a young man he had lived it up—not that he had ever told her about his escapades; he was too discreet. But servants, especially old retainers, talked.

"You're awake then." Her mother's harsh voice interrupted Yvette's thoughts. The older woman limped into the room, the ever present black shawl about her shoulders and a string of pearls at her throat. She leaned heavily on the silver-tipped stick.

"I didn't think it was a crime to lie down in the afternoon," said Yvette. "This place is such a drag."

"You should be out in the fresh air. You could swim in the lake or go boating, instead of moping around up here."

"I don't feel like it. I'm bored."

"No doubt you are, after the kind of life I imagine you lead when in Paris!" Juliette's voice was acid.

"It's my life!"

"As you so frequently say. What's wrong with you? Where's the American?"

"I don't know."

"You have quarreled?" And when Yvette did not answer: "All right. You do not have to tell me. I've seen that sulky expression too often."

"All right, so we've quarreled," said Yvette savagely.

"What about?"

"Does it matter?"

Juliette eyed her shrewdly. "Why should I not ask questions? I am your mother—although you seem to forget it at times. Besides, in the past you have always complained that I showed no interest in you. Now that I do, you are angry." She shrugged. "I don't profess to understand the modern generation, and I don't think I want to, but why can't you have a pleasant manner, like the English girl?"

"Don't talk to me about *her!*"

"Oh-ho, so that's it!" said Juliette, with a note of triumph in her voice. "You've quarreled because of Ann."

"Very well, if you must know—*yes!*"

"He is in love with her?"

"He *thinks* he is." Yvette turned away irritably, lit another cigarette.

"You are so quick tempered, so impetuous! Oh, you stupid child. Why do you behave like this? You know that she will not be with us much longer."

Yvette's eyes flickered uneasily. "I don't like her. No . . . I really hate her. And I want her away from here! But I don't want her to be . . . murdered."

"There is no other way. If there were I would have chosen it. When she is gone all your troubles will be over. Now come, let us go downstairs. You know your papa hates to be kept waiting for his meals."

Pierre Duval ate hurriedly as usual, gulping down his food as though it were his last meal. He talked with his mouth full, masticating noisily, ignoring the grimaces of his wife and daughter. He spoke about how pleased he was with the progress that Ann was making.

He patted his lips with the crumpled napkin leaning to one side and beamed at Ann from the far end of the dining table. His breath caused the nearest candle flame to flicker so shadows danced on the walls of the lofty dining room.

"You are a very fast typist, Ann. I can see that we have—how do you call it, a treasure in you?"

Ann flushed prettily. "It is kind of you to say so."

"If you continue to work at this pace I see no reason why, in a few days' time, you cannot return to your friends. Unless, of course, you prefer to stay here?" He shot his wife a quick glance. "I suppose there would be no objection to Ann staying on if she wished?"

"Of course not," said Juliette, nodding agreement. "But she might prefer to live out."

Yvette said, "Naturally she would sooner live out. I know I would!"

"Well, I do find it rather quiet here," Ann admitted.

"But yes, I understand." Duval beamed at her. "And we are old, my wife and I . . . in any case, you would have your evenings free to do as you wished. No, we must keep to our original arrangement, that this should only be for a few days." He got to his feet. "Now, if you will excuse me, I have work to do. But you need not hurry, Ann. There is plenty of time."

"And no nonsense this evening, Pierre," Juliette said crisply. "Ann may deny it, but you frightened her the other evening—and it's not surprising."

Duval looked indignant. "I'm quite all right," he said, but his eyes had a glassy look, as though another of his curious attacks were imminent.

Yvette said casually, "Has Steve phoned you today, Ann?"

Ann was surprised at the question. "Why, no."

"I saw him this morning. You didn't mind my seeing him, I suppose?"

"Why should I?"

"I was merely helping him with his research."

"I see." Ann looked at her coolly. "What made you think he would telephone me?" She must not let Yvette see that her words had disturbed her.

She must trust Steve. She believed that she could.

Yvette colored. An older, more experienced girl might have used the trip to the ruined chateau to arouse her rival's suspicions, to make her jealous. A hint here and there would have been all that was needed. But Yvette was too anxious to know if Ann had heard of their quarrel.

"We . . . we had a . . . disagreement," she managed to say, trying to sound casual.

"I'm sorry," said Ann, still in a cool voice. "You surprise me. Steve has never struck me as the kind of man to quarrel."

"It was my fault," said Yvette. "I started it."

Ann pushed back her plate and folded her napkin. She wondered what was coming next.

Juliette shot her daughter a venomous glance, as though afraid of what she would say. "You are not, I trust, going to say anything that will embarrass Ann," she said tartly. "She is after all a guest in our house. Really, Yvette, there are times when you positively appal me."

"I wasn't going to 'embarrass' her, as you put it," Yvette snapped. "I just wanted to apologize—to her and to Steve."

Ann was startled. "Apologize? For what?" she asked.

"I knew you were fond of him," said Yvette. "And I deliberately—what do you say, set my cap for him?"

137

"And?" asked Ann intrigued. Her heart was thumping, and she wondered what had happened between this evil girl and Steve.

Yvette's eyes were mocking her now. "You needn't look so worried . . . nothing happened."

"Knowing Steve, I'm sure it didn't," said Ann flatly.

"He wasn't interested," said Yvette, and Juliette was breathing heavily. "Apparently he's a one-girl man," Yvette added derisively. Then she looked contrite. "I'm sorry. I shouldn't speak like that. The fact is, we had a quarrel, and I said some rather unpleasant things. I want to say I'm sorry—to you and to Steve."

Ann was puzzled. She could guess what it had cost the other girl to raise the subject, much less to apologize. But it was all so very much out of character. Yvette was hard and brittle; she wasn't the apologetic kind. What was she up to?

Ann said, "I'm sure you're grossly exaggerating it all, Yvette. Whatever it was, no doubt Steve has forgotten all about it. He's so busy, you know, he just hasn't time for trivialities." She rose. "Now, if you'll excuse me . . ."

And I hope that put you in your place, you little minx, she thought as she left the table, conscious of Yvette's burning gaze.

As she entered her office the telephone jangled.

Would that be Steve? She lifted the receiver eagerly.

"Ann?" Steve's voice crackled over the line. "I must see you. It's important."

"What's wrong?" she asked anxiously.

"I can't tell you over the telephone," he said. "But it's vital that I see you. Can you meet me at the boathouse tonight, at nine o'clock?"

"I suppose so," she said puzzled. "But won't you tell me—"

"When I see you," said Steve, and before she could formulate any more questions, he had hung up.

Ann wondered about his brief call for the remainder of the day, which seemed to drag leadenly. But nine o'clock came at last and it was exactly on the hour when she reached the boathouse. There had been no difficulty about leaving the chateau; as usual, she had been working on her own all evening and would not be missed. The night was cool, and the breeze was fresh and pleasant on her brow; the lake stretched away before her, silent and silvery in the pale light of the moon. She hoped that Steve would not be long; it would be wonderful to see him again, to feel his arms about her. And she had so much to tell him.

She was tempted to smoke, then decided against it. The glow of the cigarette might be seen from the chateau, and someone might come to investigate.

When ten restless minutes had passed and fifteen became twenty, she began to worry. What had happened to delay Steve? His voice had sounded so urgent over the telephone.

Her restlessness changed to uneasiness and then suddenly to alarm when a man stepped out from the bushes—a portly bearded man whom she recognized instantly. And in his hand was a gun, leveled at her stomach.

"Please don't cry out, Miss Preston," he said. "I don't want to hurt you, but I shan't hesitate to use this gun if necessary."

Chapter Eleven

At about the same time that Ann was still typing in her office puzzling about Steve's message, Vorrelli was standing in his small living room, his eyes fixed anxiously on the door. Every now and then he would walk to the window and stare out, alternately glancing at the heavy gold watch on his wrist.

What the devil had happened to Max? He had been gone nearly twenty-four hours, and there had been no sign of him. He had waited outside with the car for a long time, expecting every moment to see his companion reappear. In the end, wondering what had gone wrong, and not daring to wait any longer in case somebody spotted the car, Vorrelli had gone home.

All next day he had waited, hourly expecting Max to turn up. In the end he had realized there was only one thing to do: go and look for him. Obviously Max had met with some sort of an accident; perhaps part of the ruined wing had fallen on him, burying him. In any case, he could stand the suspense no longer.

He took one last glance around the room then switched off the light and went out. It was a pleasant, starlit night, and his feet made no sound as he trudged up the lane, crossed the quiet country road with its leafy trees, and struck off through a small copse toward the grim stone pile that was the chateau. He had decided against using the car—at least until he knew what had happened to Max; a car was too easily seen.

He skirted the old boathouse with its wooden landing stage and moved with greater caution, creeping from bush to bush until at last he was standing in the shadows beneath the crumbling walls of the west wing. His eyes flickered left and right, searching the darkness. A heavy Luger was clasped in his pudgy fist, and it gave him comfort. He didn't intend to be taken by surprise.

When he came to the bushes which concealed a hole in the wall, he paused. He glanced about him, his eyes cold and hard. Silence. There was only a slight breeze to stir the trees; it was as though the night itself watched and waited.

He crawled through and switched on the flashlight he held in his left hand. He crept forward through the cellar, sweeping the light from side to side. Five minutes passed before he came to a door in a brick wall. He swore.

The door had been open on his previous visit; now it was locked and bolted. He swore again viciously, the obscenities bubbling from his thick lips. He carried nothing to force the lock, not even a penknife. Max would have found it easy. Using the gun would be much too noisy. He began to look around for something he could utilize.

The powerful flashlight beam slid slowly over the floor of the cellar. There were piles of rubble, plaster, worm-eaten beams, joists. Something gray and furry with beady red eyes darted away in the darkness, and Vorrelli jumped.

The light moved on, came to rest on another mound of junk, stopped. Vorrelli's breath escaped in a low moan between his teeth.

A human hand was protruding from beneath some crumbled bricks and blackened beams!

He moved closer. There was a blue smudge on one of the fingers beside the thick gold band. Paint. There was absolutely no doubt about who was crushed beneath the weight of those heavy old timbers.

Vorrelli stared for a long time. He could tell that this had not been an accident. Max had been murdered, and a clumsy, probably hasty attempt was made to conceal his body. Sweat gleamed on Vorrelli's forehead as he looked at that stiffened, grotesquely upthrust hand.

Then he grunted. At least he knew now what had happened to Max; if he'd known before he could have saved himself a long and anxious wait. There was nothing he could do; it would be too dangerous to try to break into the chateau. He must wait for Miguel—or he would have to try to get the girl himself.

She must surely leave the chateau soon; they couldn't keep her there permanently. Sooner or later she would want to go out, if only into the garden—perhaps tonight. Time was now getting desperately short. The Duvals couldn't allow her to remain alive much longer. He must think of something—some way to reach her.

Suddenly his eyes narrowed. There *was* a way. He had met her on the plane; that made it easier. He would pose as a friend, tell her she was in danger. He smiled, but the smile never reached his cold eyes.

He retraced his steps and a few minutes later emerged from the hole in the wall. From there he made his way toward the boathouse; from the chateau a thin line of light edged the draped windows of the second-floor lounge, but the room where Ann worked was in darkness. She must have gone to bed early. Never mind; he would telephone her first thing in the morning. . . .

Suddenly he glimpsed a movement in the shadows and, instinctively, he dived for the bushes. Somebody was standing in the darkness beside the boathouse.

Then a thin hiss of triumph escaped his lips. It was Ann Preston!

It was then that he quickly stepped forward, the gun held firmly in his hand.

Ann looked at Vorrelli steadily, trying to hide her fear. "What do you want?" she asked, but in spite of her efforts her voice shook slightly.

"Just the answer to a few questions." He gestured with the gun. "Move around to the other side of the boathouse, so that we can't be seen."

Ann tried to keep a grip on her rising fear. Somehow she must keep the man talking, keep him here until Steve came.

"All right," she said. "But if you try to harm me—"

"Relax. You've nothing to be scared of, as long as you do as you're told and answer my questions."

"Very well."

She backed away from him and round to the side of the boathouse. From beyond came a small knocking sound which startled her at first until she realized it was a boat rocking gently against its moorings.

Vorrelli followed her, three yards behind. His sunglasses were in his breast pocket, and his large, protuberant eyes were cold and unblinking.

"Okay," he said nasally. "Where's the stuff?"

"I'm sorry. I don't know what you mean."

"The loot."

"I still don't understand!"

"Quit stalling, Miss Preston! You know what I'm talking about."

"But I don't!" she protested. "There must be some mistake."

"You know Big French?"

"Who?"

His voice hardened. "Big French Duval."

"If you mean Monsieur Duval—" If only Steve would come! What had delayed him? He had said nine o'clock, and it was well past that now. Had anything happened? She couldn't bear to think of the possibility and thrust it quickly from her mind.

"I don't mean him. You know darn well I don't! I'm talking about Big French. According to my information, you know him very well."

She shook her head emphatically, her eyes fixed almost hypnotically upon the gleaming gun. "I tell you, I've no idea what you're talking about! I don't know anybody named Big—Big French. Now—if you'll excuse me I'm getting cold, and I'd like to go back indoors."

"Not so fast," said Vorrelli grimly. "You don't fool me."

"I'll be missed," said Ann breathlessly. "I told

them I was just going for a walk around the grounds. Somebody will come looking for me in a minute or two."

"Let 'em come," he said. "They'll be sorry if they do." He moved the gun menacingly. "Meanwhile, start walking."

Fear swelled in her throat. "What are you going to do with me?" she asked through dry lips.

"You'll see. You're going to take a little walk with me—to my place. You're going to meet a friend of mine."

She shrank back, no longer trying to hide her terror. "No! no!"

"A very persuasive man is my friend Miguel. Like his name implies, he's got Mexican blood. He's more Mex than anything you see on the movies. He's for real—a refined man, you might think, but that's just a cover-up, as you'll find out." He went on conversationally. "He can be very persuasive indeed. I guess having Indians for neighbors, as you might say, was kind of—enlightening. Now, start walking. And no funny business!"

Numbly Ann turned and led the way through the trees, hearing the man's heavy footsteps behind her. Fear ate away at the edges of her mind. What was all this about? What did he mean by loot? Had he mistaken her for somebody else. But he must have; surely he would realize his mistake!

Where was Steve? What had delayed him?

Where was this man taking her? And what would happen when he brought her face to face with his friend, Miguel? Did he really mean to imply that she would be . . . tortured?

Her veins felt as though ice were running through them. She had never been so frightened in her life; it was as much as she could do to put one foot in front of the other.

Then, suddenly, she heard a muttered exclamation, followed by a curse and the sound of a struggle. She whirled round, her hands flying to her throat, her fears swept away. Steve!

Two dark figures were locked together behind her, swaying back and forth. But one of them broke free and ran blindly away through the trees. The other man picked himself up and lurched toward her.

"Oh, Steve!" Ann cried. "Thank God you came!"

Then the words froze on her lips. It wasn't Steve! In the light of the moon that filtered through the leaves she found herself gazing up into the gaunt, sunken features of Raymonde.

"Are you all right, m'amselle?" He loomed over her. His eyes seemed even deeper set in that pale light. He wore a long black coat, and there was a dark silk scarf around his neck. "You shouldn't be out here." He sounded reproachful. "What happened?"

"I—I came out for some fresh air and—"

He interrupted her. "You were expecting to meet somebody, I think?"

She bit her lip. "I was expecting to meet St— Mr. Martin." There was no point in denying it, for she had called his name when she ran toward Raymonde.

He looked at her thoughtfully. He scratched the side of his face, seeming to have something on his mind. His eyes had a faraway look.

"Then you haven't seen him?"

"No. He promised to be here at nine o'clock."

"The man who attacked you? You would know him again?"

"Oh yes! He came over on the plane with me."

He looked at her sharply. "It was the American who has been hanging around the chateau?"

She nodded.

"Do you know where he was taking you?"

"No, but I got the impression it wasn't far. He was—he was asking me a lot of questions, and because I couldn't answer them—I didn't even know what he was talking about!—he said he would take me to a friend of his named Miguel."

"A friend?" Raymonde looked startled. "And what kind of questions were they?"

She frowned. "I couldn't understand what he was getting at. Something about loot and a man named Big French. He seemed to think I knew him and knew too where the loot was hidden."

The gaunt-faced butler took her arm. "I think we had better return to the house. As I said, it's not wise to wander about the grounds after dark."

Once in the kitchen he told her to sit down while he made her a hot drink. "I suggest you go to bed now," he said quietly.

"I haven't thanked you yet for—"

"It is nothing," he muttered.

"Do you think he is the man who attacked that girl in the village?" Ann asked suddenly. "Shouldn't we inform the police?"

"He is not the man," said Raymonde grimly. "Other attacks were made before he came. Now, you had better go to bed and rest. You've had a frightening experience."

But when Ann finally went up to her room she found it difficult to sleep. Who was the American? What was he after? And, more important, *what had happened to Steve?* Why hadn't he kept the all-important appointment?

She determined that no matter what happened, tomorrow she would find out.

When Yvette had left Steve stranded against the old ruined chateau, he had made his way back to the village, with no kind thoughts about her in his mind. He had spent the day searching for Vorrelli, and discreet enquiries had finally culminated in his locating the villa that the American had leased from the Biarritz agents. Returning to his hotel that evening, Steve had showered and changed and given a great deal of thought to a cable which had arrived from Washington.

Later, following a casual meeting with the local garage proprietor, he had gone hurrying back to the hotel to telephone Ann.

"There's no doubt about it, m'sieu," the garage proprietor had told him. "I was in the resistance during the war. I have done such a thing myself. A few nuts loosened, that is all there is to do. When the car goes down a steep hill the brakes give under the strain and it is all over."

At around seven o'clock, Steve had hurried out to his hired car, his good-looking sharply-cut features unusually stern. He had driven out of the village, the mechanic's words still drumming in his head.

"She's got to leave that place," he told himself grimly. "If I have to drag her out by her hair!"

That wasn't all. Something was worrying Ann too; he could tell from the tone of her voice when she answered him on the telephone. Well, they'd straighten everything out when they met, but one thing was certain: she would pack her bags and leave the chateau right away—and to hell with the Duvals! He wasn't going to let her stay another minute in the place.

Somebody had deliberately loosened the nuts in Yvette's car—and Ann had been driving it. Why, he didn't know. He only knew that she was in the gravest danger. And when he told her what the mechanic had told him, she would realize that it would be folly to stay at the chateau, no matter what pleas or excuses her employers put forward.

He glanced at his watch. Eight o'clock. That didn't give him much time for what he had to do. . . .

Two miles from the chateau he left the main, tree-lined road and turned up a narrow track. It was deeply rutted, the ground baked hard by the sun, and the car springs creaked protestingly. A hundred yards along the lane he turned into a field, swung in a full circle, and braked. It might be necessary later to be facing the right way; it could mean the difference between life and death.

He went out into the lane. It was dark now; black clouds scudded by overhead; there was rain in the air. Five more minutes and he came to the villa where Vorrelli was staying.

It was set back from the lane and was of average size, with a veranda and steps leading down to a square sandy garden. The place was in darkness, but the shutters had not been closed. Somewhere in the distance he heard waves washing against the beach. There was a strong smell of seaweed and burning wood. This was not the only holiday villa near the dunes.

He crouched in the bushes, watchful.

When nothing stirred, he circled the building. There was a small wooden shed and an outhouse in an adjoining rickety lean-to. He looked again toward the green-tiled roof. No lights; no movement.

Damn them in Washington! Why hadn't they cabled sooner, instead of sitting on their backsides dreaming? Shove 'em in the field; they'd soon learn to think and act fast, You had to—otherwise it was the silent ride to the graveyard—always assuming you weren't dropped over the side of a launch, embracing an iron bar. The silent grave or the hungry fish. . . .

The three wooden steps creaked beneath his weight as he crept up to the veranda. He reached a window; the curtains were closely drawn, so he couldn't see inside.

He tapped on the back door lightly. No response. He took a narrow strip of plastic from his inside pocket, and moments later the lock clicked back and the door opened. He stepped inside, listening intently.

Silence.

He shone his flashlight around the barren

kitchen. Two cups containing dregs of coffee stood on the draining board. There was a small square hall beyond; doors were open.

The lounge was to his left. It was long and poorly furnished with a heavy, old-fashioned sideboard, easy chairs, rugs and highly polished flooring. A table stood in the window; on it there was an unfinished watercolor painting, a tin of paints, and a crumpled packet of Gauloises.

He pulled out the sideboard drawers, riffling through the papers they contained, mostly bills from the local tradesmen, some travel folders, and a map of the district. He thrust the drawers back and crossed the small hall to the bedroom.

It was then he felt the quick rush of air. He sidestepped, but not quickly enough. Something caught him with almost paralyzing force on the shoulder. He jerked his head quickly to one side, pain shrieking through him, and tried to grapple with the dark figure lurking there.

He saw a flash of very white teeth as a second blow slammed against his head. A thousand multicolored lights exploded before his eyes, and that was the last thing he knew. . . .

Chapter Twelve

"The police must be informed immediately!" Pierre Duval exclaimed indignantly. "I told you that bearded man was hanging about and up to no good!"

It was breakfast the following morning. They were all there, Juliette, Pierre Duval, Ann and Yvette. Duval sat at the far end of the table in the lofty, gloomy dining room. He was wearing his dressing gown and was brandishing his fork; his face was flushed.

"There is no need to excite yourself," Juliette said calmly.

Duval was breathing heavily. His eyes were round and bright.

"I am not exciting myself!" he squeaked.

"It doesn't look like it, does it?" muttered Yvette.

"Don't you talk like that!" her mother snapped.

Ann had come down to breakfast to discover

that Raymonde had already told them of the attack on her the previous night.

"I don't see what complaining to the police will do. They still haven't caught the man who attacked the girl from the village," Juliette noted.

"It's our duty to—" began Duval.

"He'll be miles away by this time," Yvette interjected.

"That's not the point," her father said testily. For once he seemed determined to have his own way. "Men like that are a menace!"

Juliette said coldly, "Of course, it is entirely up to Ann; she had the unpleasant experience. But you know as well as I do what this will mean, Pierre. The police will be here in full force, wasting our time asking questions, poking into this and that."

It was, reflected Ann, almost as though Juliette wanted to make sure that the police did not visit the chateau. She was reminded of an earlier suspicion: Was Juliette hiding someone in the west wing? Was that the reason she did not want the police on the premises? Had the occupant of the deserted wing attacked and killed the man Ann had seen lying in the pool in the cellar?

"Look, my dear," Juliette said turning to Ann. "You'll be constantly interrupted; it will put you days behind when you have done so well up to now. Only last night we were saying that another two days, and you should be able to return to your friends, the Langognes."

"Yes," Duval agreed almost reluctantly. "That is true."

"Anyway, I don't think the person who attacked Ann was the same man who attacked that girl from the village," Yvette said. She turned to look at Ann. "You say he questioned you?"

Ann brushed her lips with her napkin. "He seemed to think I knew the whereabouts of some money—the loot, he called it. I simply didn't know what he was talking about."

"He was probably just a drunk," Yvette remarked. "Thought perhaps we had a lot of money in the house. Don't you think so, mama?"

"Very likely," Juliette said and looked thoughtfully from one to the other. Then her cold eyes fastened on Ann's face, searching it. "Was that all he said?"

"Yes. It hadn't occurred to me that he might be after whatever money he thought would be here in the chateau."

Juliette seemed puzzled. "But what else could he have meant?"

Ann bit her lip. Yes, what else could he have meant? She had not missed the quick glance that Juliette and Yvette had exchanged during the time they were first discussing the attack on her. She was more and more convinced that they were hiding something from her. Moreover, she had a feeling that Raymonde was also suspicious; also she felt that he was on her side and not the Duvals'.

If only she could see Steve! She was still wondering what could have happened to prevent him from keeping their appointment—the appointment he had stressed was so urgent.

And why hadn't he telephoned? Either last night, or first thing this morning? She wondered if she could ask for time off to go down to the village, if only to set her mind at rest.

She said, "I think the police *should* be informed. As Monsieur Duval says, the man could attack somebody else."

Juliette's face darkened.

"Very well," she said stiffly. "It's your own time you will be wasting. I will telephone the inspector this morning. No doubt he will come here to question you later on."

Yvette flicked the cigarette ash from the Gauloise she was smoking. "A bit stupid of you to be wandering around the chateau at that time of night, wasn't it?" she said. "I mean you *had* been warned that somebody was going about attacking people."

Ann flushed. "I felt like some fresh air before going to bed. After all, I'd been cooped up indoors all day."

Yvette's hard eyes appraised her thoughtfully.

Ann suspected that she did not believe her, but she no longer cared. She was sick of this house and the odd behavior of its inhabitants. However much she tried to conceal it, Juliette disliked her too. And Yvette was openly hostile. Well, she'd had enough. She didn't have to stay; she would leave at the end of the week. Steve and Tom had been right: this was no place for her.

Yvette said, "You wouldn't catch me wandering about down by the boathouse—not unless I was meeting someone." The inference was obvious.

"But who would Ann be meeting by the boathouse?" demanded Pierre Duval with a note of petulance in his voice.

Yvette looked bored. "I don't know, and I'm sure I don't care."

Oh yes, you do, thought Ann. You're waiting for me to say it was Steve—but I'm not going to.

"Whatever Ann's reasons were," Juliette said, "I am sure they are entirely her own affair. After all, it's quite true that since that visit to the village —which might have ended so disastrously—she hadn't been out of the house. You drive her too hard, Pierre," she added accusingly.

He gave a sweeping gesture with his arm.

"Can I help it if there is so much work?" he asked contritely. "It is Paris who makes the work, demanding this, demanding that!"

"You should be a more considerate employer.

Look at the girl; she has lost most of the color she had when she came here. There are dark smudges beneath her eyes. It is all too clear that she is overworked and not getting enough fresh air."

"I must confess I could do with a break," said Ann. This was surely her chance. "Perhaps it would be a good idea if I went to the village and reported to the police myself? It would save you from being worried too much." At the same time, she might be able to find Steve.

"No, don't do that!" said Juliette quickly—a little too quickly. "In any case, it isn't possible; Yvette's car is still at the garage undergoing repair, and the battery of my husband's car is dead."

"I could catch the bus," said Ann.

"You have just missed the early one, my dear, I'm afraid."

"Oh dear." Ann could not conceal her disappointment. She was quick to see a flicker of pleasure on Yvette's face.

"No—leave it to me," Juliette said reaching for her stick and rising to her feet. "I will telephone this morning. The inspector can come out here, and it will perhaps save much time and get everything over quickly."

Duval had also risen; his eyes were gleaming.

"I know," he began triumphantly.

"You know what?" asked Juliette, her voice still cold.

"Why should Ann be deprived of a chance to get some fresh air?"

"And what about her work?"

"What's to stop her from typing in the summerhouse?" the little man exclaimed. "Look, it is a sunny morning and quite warm. I have always found it very cozy there."

"It would be a change from working alone in that room, I have to agree," said Juliette grudgingly. She looked at Ann. "It is up to you, of course."

"I'd welcome a change," said Ann. "But isn't the summerhouse on the other side of the lake?"

"It's a long walk around it," said Yvette.

"You're so lazy," said her mother. "I think it is a very good idea."

"But it's not necessary for you to walk, Ann," smiled Duval. "You can use the launch. You would be across the lake in no time. Well, that's settled then. I'll put the typewriter and paper aboard—and a flask of hot coffee as well."

Ann smiled. "Thank you very much, Monsieur Duval. It was wonderful of you to think of it."

He clapped his hands boyishly. "You will love the summerhouse. You cannot help but enjoy working there on a morning such as this. Shall we say about ten o'clock?"

She thanked him again and went into her office, closing the door behind her. She sat down at her desk and picked up the local telephone directory. She turned the pages, then began to run her finger down the list of names.

Steve was probably still having breakfast. It would be easy for him to visit her at the summerhouse. Nobody need know, and they could talk together in private. There was a lot she wanted to tell him. At least, she reflected with a faint smile, he would be delighted to know that she proposed giving them notice. He had never wanted her to work there in the first place.

Ah, here it was . . . Hôtel Continentale.

She lifted the receiver. Waited. She jiggled the receiver up and down. That's odd. For a country line the operator was usually prompt to answer.

She listened intently, but there was no sound at all.

There was no doubt about it: the line was dead. . . .

"Don't worry about the phone," Pierre Duval told her, when she reported that the line was out of order. "I already know. Raymonde will go on his bicycle to the nearest kiosk and ask for an engineer to be sent as soon as possible."

Bitterly disappointed, Ann prepared to take her work out to the summerhouse. It would have been an ideal opportunity to meet Steve and talk with him. Now it was impossible; working by the lake had suddenly lost much of its appeal.

But she couldn't very well say that she had changed her mind. With luck the telephone would be repaired by the time she returned for lunch, and she could try to contact Steve then.

"I've put the portable and everything you'll need in the launch," Duval said cheerfully. His round face was wreathed in smiles. "And, of course, the coffee."

"You're very kind," said Ann forcing a smile.

"You'll find it very cozy," he said as they reached the boathouse together. "Warm—glass, you see. And no drafts."

The small launch was already moored to the wooden landing stage. It was not unlike the craft she had once hired for an hour on the Broads.

"Now you're sure you will be all right?" he asked anxiously when he had explained the controls to her. When she nodded he said cheerfully, "Then we'll see you later for lunch." He went off with a friendly wave of his hand.

Ann was a little nervous at first but her confidence grew as she became accustomed to the controls, which were simple enough. After all, there wasn't so much difference in driving a launch and a car. All she needed to do to increase speed was to draw the throttle lever toward her; there were only two gears, forward and reverse.

Growing bolder, she increased speed, thrilling to the white, creamy waves rising on either side of the bows. She relaxed more in the seat; it was comfortable behind the windshield, the fine spray splashing against the side windows.

It was really exhilarating, so Ann decided to travel the length of the lake, swing around in a wide arc, and return on the far side, pulling in beside the landing stage below the cream-and-green-painted summerhouse. Wild fowl scattered, wings beating. The stench of rotting weeds mingled with the warm oily smell of the engine. She steered well clear of the swaying patches of weeds and again increased speed.

The brown water swirled and eddied, the launch began to bump and roll. Don't get overconfident, she told herself warningly.

She was turning when she realized that the launch was losing speed and reacting sluggishly to the controls. Now the hot engine fumes were catching at her throat.

With rising alarm she realized that the little cockpit was becoming stiflingly hot; the pungent odor of the oil was stronger. The engine must be overheated! She slipped into neutral to let it cool off. It was probably some time since the launch had been used, and some fault could have developed.

It was then she felt the sudden chill at her feet.

She glanced down startled, and the color drained from her cheeks.

Brown, muddy water was swirling about her ankles!

She glanced quickly behind her, along the length of the launch, and was aghast at what she saw. It was rapidly filling with water, rising every passing second. She looked around desperately, searching for something with which to bale out the water.

The launch was sinking lower and lower into the lake! The coffee flask floated against her knees, and the typing paper was awash.

Her eyes switched to the tree-lined bank. There was no one in sight. In her imagination the bent, misshapen tree branches seemed to mock her. Even the sun had disappeared behind the clouds, and the icy water creeping up to her thighs chilled her to the bone.

"Help! Help!"

She screamed now, again and again. The launch lurched alarmingly. The water was gushing in over the gunwales. It rolled sideways suddenly and, Ann, caught off-balance, was flung into the lake.

She plunged beneath the muddy surface, sinking down and down into the darkness. Tendrils of weeds like ghostly fingers brushed against her legs. There was a dreadful hammering in her head, a red mist swirled before her eyes. She struck out madly, crazily, clawing her way up through the water. Oh God, would she never reach the surface! She kicked out wildly, her lungs feeling as though they would burst, the drumming in her head threatening to burst her skull like an overripe orange.

Then she reached the surface and was sucking air into her tortured lungs. But terror still gripped her throat; she was merely prolonging her own agony, for she could not swim.

She fought to keep her head above water, shouting with all the strength left to her: "Help! Help!"

Water spilled into her eyes, into her open mouth. She gulped, spit out water, struggled insanely. She couldn't keep afloat any longer. She was sinking! She could no longer see, and her lungs were filling with water, bursting, ready to explode. She flung up her hands; her legs were like dead weights pulling her down, down. She had no strength left now . . .

Then something fastened about her right shoulder. From a long way off she seemed to hear a voice: "Don't fight me! Don't struggle!"

She felt herself being hauled over onto her back, was vaguely conscious of being pulled backward, the muddy water splashing over her face. She seemed to be floating . . . floating on cotton which soon turned into something hard and solid beneath her shoulders.

Barely conscious she realized that now her rescuer had turned her over on her face on the ground and was applying artificial respiration. She coughed up water, choked and sputtered, felt her lungs filling with air, her head clearing. At last she was able to turn and see over her shoulder.

"Tom!" she cried.

"Take it easy, dear," he said gently. "You're going to be all right now."

With his arm about her shoulders, she sat up and stared blankly around her. She had been lying on the floor of what she guessed to be the summerhouse. There were a couple of deck chairs propped against the wall, a table, a wooden chair, and a pot with a dead plant in it.

Her gaze returned to Tom's anxious face.

"I don't know what to say. You . . . saved my life, Tom!" she said.

"Forget it, Ann." He flushed. "There's a blanket on that bench; better wrap it around you, and get out of those wet things. Then we'll go back to the chateau."

He stood up and went out, and she began to strip, pulling off her wet, clinging clothes. When he came back carrying his jacket, she was wrapped in the blanket.

He lit two cigarettes and handed one to her.

"Bless you, Tom," she said, still rather shakily. "You saved my life. I'll never forget."

"Forget it," he said gruffly.

"How did you happen to be here, just at the right time?" she asked. "I thought you were in Rouen."

"I got back last night. I heard about your accident with the car, and I was worried. I tried to phone you but it was out of order or something, so I came right over. Thank God I did!" He added, "You know, of course, that when the brakes failed it was because they'd been tampered with. Somebody deliberately tried to kill you."

His expression was grim. He was wearing a striped shirt that clung to him like a second skin, emphasizing his broad shoulders and muscular chest. There were wisps of fair hair on his arms. Ann thought, not for the first time, that he looked like a farmer rather than a scientist.

"And this business with the boat—it was obviously another attempt to get rid of you. Did they know you couldn't swim?"

"Why, yes. I believe I mentioned it—the first day I came," Ann stammered. "You're sure about the brakes, Tom?"

"Positive. I called the garage last night. There's no mistake about it."

"But why would any of the Duval family want to kill me?" Ann asked, thinking that surely Yvette's jealousy over Steve would not carry her to such extremes!

"I don't know." He shrugged his shoulders. "But you're not staying here a moment longer."

"I wonder . . . I wonder if that bearded man has anything to do with it," said Ann.

"What bearded man?"

She told him of the attack on her at the boathouse the previous evening. "It must be him," she said. "I can't believe the Duvals would . . ."

"It doesn't make sense," he said shaking his head. "The reason that man accosted you was obviously to get information from you. He wouldn't try to kill you—not before he'd got what he wanted, anyway."

Ann bit her underlip. Tom was right, of course. So it must be the Duvals who were behind these attempts on her life. But *why?* What possible reason could they have?

"You must go to the police," he said.

She hesitated. "There's no proof," she said. "The brakes *could* have been an accident, so could the boat. Besides, if you're right, and they do want me out of the way, then I've a right to know why!"

"Oh, for heaven's sake!" he burst out irritably. "You're not some tough heroine in a TV series. This is for real. Something's going on—and maybe that's the reason Steve Martin has disappeared."

Ann's heart seemed to miss a beat. "Steve? Disappeared?" she asked.

"I went to his hotel this morning before coming here. I was worried about this brake business. I thought you might have seen him, and I was anxious to know how you were. I was told his bed hadn't been slept in. Apparently he'd had a drink in the bar last evening, made a phone call and gone out."

"He telephoned me, asking me to meet him at the boathouse at nine o'clock. But he didn't turn up. It was while I was waiting for him that I was . . . attacked."

Tom was silent for a moment, then he said, "It fits. It could have been a frame-up—I mean, Steve and the man who attacked you are both Americans."

She was shocked. "I'll never believe that!" she said fiercely. "Besides, it doesn't explain Steve's disappearance."

"Unless he skipped when he found out the attack on you had failed."

"I won't have you saying such things about him, Tom! I *know* he's on the level. Like you, he's been trying to persuade me to leave this place."

He scratched his head. "Well, if the man who attacked you has got nothing to do with the Duvals, then it would seem you've got two enemies. Anyway, you're coming home with me."

Ann shook her head. There was a glint in her

eyes that had not been there earlier, and her mouth was tightly set.

"No," she said flatly. "If somebody is trying to kill me, I want to know why! Don't you see, Tom? *If* Steve found out what the Duvals were trying to do—and that was probably the reason he wanted to meet me last night—they might have captured him. He might even be a prisoner in the chateau at this very moment!"

"On the other hand, that bearded chap might know something about his whereabouts. I still think we ought to go to the police, Ann."

"No!" Ann grabbed his arm. "If Steve *is* a prisoner somewhere, then going to the police might put his life in danger. If they killed him—"

"But look here, Ann."

She went on firmly, "You could make enquiries, Tom—discreetly, I mean. You might manage to pick up some clue, get a lead as to what might have happened to him. Meantime, I'll search the chateau. Will you do that, Tom? Please!" She looked at him pleadingly.

"You're . . . you're very fond of him, aren't you?" Tom asked quietly.

"Yes. I'm sorry, Tom—I'd do anything rather than hurt you . . . but you see how it is. I can't help myself."

He squeezed her and gave her a cheerful affectionate smile. "Forget it, Ann. It's okay. I'll nose around."

"You'll be careful?"

"Trust me. But I still don't like the idea of your going back to that damned chateau!"

"They won't try anything again so soon. And in any case, I'll be on my guard from now on."

They parted. Ann, carrying her sodden clothes and still wrapped in the blanket, began the long walk around the lake back to the chateau. Her mind was seething with doubt, anxiety, and fear. But her fear was more for Steve now than for herself. Had the Duvals actually imprisoned him in the chateau?

She remembered the body she had seen floating facedown in the cellar pool and shuddered. Nothing, she thought determinedly, would induce her to leave the chateau now—not until she had found Steve.

Chapter Thirteen

Juliette Duval's dark eyes gleamed with triumph as she turned away from the window of the second-floor lounge. An hour before she had seen Ann get aboard the launch and draw away from the landing stage.

Now there was no sign of the launch.

As always there was a big fire blazing in the hearth. Logs spat, and showers of sparks disappeared up the wide chimney. The lid of the wicker basket was open and the snake was undulating across the carpet, its tiny eyes fastened on the Frenchwoman, who was leaning heavily on her stick gazing down at the reptile affectionately.

She smiled as it slowly coiled itself around the stick, on upward over her hand to entwine itself about her arm, its unblinking, diamond-shaped eyes fastened on her, its tongue shooting in and out, less than six inches from her face.

"You are lovely, and you need loving, comforting," she crooned. "You are just like a baby." She caressed its writhing, scaly body, glanced again through the window, then limped over to the basket.

"Back to bed," she murmured. "You are making my arm numb, you silly affectionate thing. Mama has things to do." She spoke softly, and her voice held something of the tender modulation it had possessed before the terrible trapeze accident which had left her crippled for life, one leg permanently shorter than the other.

Slowly, almost reluctantly, the snake uncoiled itself and dropped into the basket. Juliette lowered the lid, glancing up as the door opened and her daughter came into the room.

Yvette gave a grimace of distaste. "You're not still playing with that horrible thing!"

"Why not?" Juliette spoke sharply. "It is the only thing in this house which gives me any affection. But let us not quarrel, Yvette, it is a time for celebration."

In the brief silence that fell upon the room the logs sputtered and a spark fell on the rug. The smell of scorched wool reached the girl's nostrils, and she stepped forward to stamp on the widening circle in the carpet.

"One of these days this dump will be burnt to the ground. And good riddance, too! You ought to burn birch—it's safer."

"Didn't you hear what I said just now?" demanded Juliette. "A time for celebration!"

"I *don't* want to hear about it," the girl said. "I've told you before . . . though perhaps she's better off. The big bang's bound to come sooner or later, the way things are going in the world today."

Before her mother could reply there came the sound of running footsteps on the stairs. The next moment Marie burst into the room. Her face was white; her eyes were black staring orbs. She was breathless, her chest heaving.

Juliette stiffened. "How dare you come in like that, Marie? Have I not told you to always knock before entering?"

"I'm sorry, madame," the girl stammered. "But there has been an accident. Ann—I mean, Miss Preston—has just come in. The launch—"

"*What?*" snapped Juliette and only Yvette noticed that she swayed a little as she spoke.

"The launch . . . it sank," said Marie. "M'amselle, she almost drowned."

The expression which came into Juliette's eyes flickered and was quickly gone. She flung up her hands. "That poor child! I will come at once. Get her to bed immediately with hot-water bottles and prepare a hot drink."

With Yvette at her side, she limped down the

stairs. Ann was standing in the hall, the blanket still wrapped about her.

"My dear child, Marie has just told me. This is dreadful! Are you all right?"

"Fortunately, yes, madame," said Ann levelly.

"Thank goodness!" Yvette sounded relieved, and Ann looked at her in surprise. That expression of relief had sounded genuine. "I'll come upstairs with you. Mother has given orders for hot-water bottles to be placed in your bed."

"Thank you, but I shall be all right," said Ann.

"How—what happened?" asked Juliette. "Marie told us the launch sank. How did you reach the shore?"

It was on the tip of Ann's tongue to mention Tom Langogne's fortuitous appearance, but she checked herself in time. It would be better if they knew nothing about Tom's presence at the chateau. If they knew that he was suspicious of them, that he was already enquiring about Steve Martin's disappearance, they might very well try to stop him too. It was better that they should think she had miraculously escaped by herself.

She said, "Fortunately the launch was near the shore. I managed to get it that far before it sank. I can't quite remember how I got to the bank. I suppose I did it somehow, or I wouldn't be here." She managed a faint smile.

Juliette looked at her intently. "But why should the launch sink?" she asked. "You did not hit anything on the water?"

"No. I've no idea what happened. One moment I was afloat, the next minute the launch was sinking."

Yvette's face was pale. "You seem to be accident prone. First the car, then the launch. But then, this place has never been particularly lucky for anyone. If you've any sense you'll leave."

"Don't talk nonsense!" Juliette shot her daughter a venomous glance. "Don't listen to her, Ann. Go up to your room and rest. I'll have a hot drink sent up to you."

"I think I will lie down for a little while," said Ann. "I feel rather shaken up."

"Of course."

"You're sure I can't be of any help?" Yvette asked. It seemed almost as though she did not want to be left alone with her mother, Ann thought. She shook her head. She was anxious to be on her own, to let her thoughts have free rein. Once in her room she gave herself a brisk rubdown until her body tingled. Then she got into bed.

When Marie came up a few minutes later with hot coffee, spiked with cognac, the maid was bubbling with excitement and anxious to talk. But Ann pretended to be too exhausted.

"Not now, Marie," she said gently. "I'll tell you all about it later."

"I understand. Of course," said the maid. She paused in the doorway on her way out. "But I did warn you, did I not? This place is bad, evil. It has a curse on it. You must get away before it is too late."

She went out, and Ann slowly sipped the welcomed coffee. It helped to relax her, and she lay back against the pillows.

Were they all involved? she thought: Juliette, Pierre, Yvette? Yet when she had been downstairs, a few moments ago, it had seemed as though Yvette had been warning her.

Pierre Duval?

It had been his suggestion that she should take the launch to the summerhouse. It would have been quite simple for him to do something which would cause the launch to sink. Yet of them all it was Pierre who seemed more friendly toward her than either his wife or daughter. She had always found him considerate, kindly, and thoughtful. And what reason could he possibly have for wanting to kill her?

There was only one answer; to be on her guard against all three of them—to keep both ears and eyes constantly open.

The coffee warmed her, made the blood quicken in her veins. Suddenly she came to a decision and sat up, swung her legs off the bed. She went to the door, opened it, and listened. All was quiet. Quickly she dressed, flinging on slacks and a shirt.

She hurried along the corridor, coming at last to Raymonde's room. There was no sound from inside, and she guessed he was in the servants' quarters. Perhaps he was out, reporting the failure of the telephone. She had a feeling now that the wire had been deliberately cut. Juliette had had no intention at all of calling in the gendarmes.

Well, at least Tom was aware of Ann's danger now, so he would not be far away.

As she reached the corridor of empty rooms, she glanced into each of them, but there was no sign of Steve. Did she really expect to find him a prisoner in the chateau? She did not know.

At last she reached the furnished room. The door was ajar and her heart pumped painfully against her ribs. She peered in. The room was empty; there was no sign that Steve had ever been there.

A wave of disappointment swept over her. She hesitated, at a loss. She had been certain that she would find him there.

Should she go back?

No—as she shone her flashlight back into the darkened corridor, she decided to continue searching. She turned stealthily into a second corridor. Her mouth was dry; the palms of her hands were moist. If the mysterious occupant of the west wing was not in his room, where was he?

The corridor opened out onto a minstrel's gallery, overlooking a large high-ceilinged hall, not unlike the gloomy dining room. It was panelled, and there was ornate scrollwork on the wide staircase which led downwards. There were gaping holes in the ceiling and roof, and she could see the sky beyond some of the heavy oak beams and rafters.

Some of the treads were missing on the stairs, and there were pools of water on the debris-littered floor. Velvet curtains hung in shreds. The vast hall smelt of dampness and decay.

Then, quite suddenly, the scent of lilies of the valley and dried leaves seemed to fill the air. With it came an awareness of evil, an overwhelming sense of impending danger.

The scent grew stronger, so strong that it caught at her throat. The aura of malignancy seemed to swirl in invisible waves about her, to close in on her, paralyzing her. She stood rooted to the floor, immobilized with terror!

Even though the sense of enveloping evil increased and tendrils of fear clutched at her heart, Ann forced herself to turn around. A gasp of unimaginable horror burst from her.

Standing in front of her, less than six yards

away, bathed in the glare of her flashlight, was a man with a horribly disfigured face.

A man? He was a living nightmare, a thing of dread! The slits that were his eyes were lost in folds of yellow flesh scarred deeply with livid red welts. The mouth was a gaping hole; one jaw was twisted and lumpy, as though it had been broken and improperly reset. His arms were flung up; the powerful hands with their thick spatulate fingers were trying to protect his eyes from the glare. Choking, animal noises came from his throat.

And then he sprang!

Ann screamed—piercingly, her eyes wide, her mouth gaping. Then she whirled and plunged wildly down the stairs, stumbling and tripping, leaping over the jagged holes in an abandon of fear, little cries bursting from her raspy throat. Reaching the bottom of the staircase she tripped over something hard and solid and fell heavily, the flashlight dropping from her hand and skittling across the wooden floor.

Sheer, unadulterated terror forced her to her feet. She ran like a demented animal, the breath gasping in and out of her mouth. Twice she fell, smashing her knees against broken furniture. Twice she clawed herself upright and ran on.

It did not occur to her to look for cover, to hide. Fear propelled her on; she could think of nothing except flight from the dreadful thing pursuing her. She blundered hysterically through the darkness.

And still he followed, guided by the noises she was making. He moved swiftly, softly, crouched, on cat's paws. He knew where every item of furniture was placed, where every hole in the floor was; he knew every inch of the dark hall. He knew that she was plunging down the center of the room. The little fool! Had she remained still she would have made it more difficult for him to find her.

But Ann's only thought was of escape—to get away from the evil-smelling hall and that unbelievably nightmarish thing!

With the breath catching in her throat, she ran on. Ahead of her, daylight streamed through a hole in the roof, and she saw that a pile of broken chairs blocked her way!

The padding footsteps grew nearer . . .

Desperately her eyes searched for something she could use as a weapon. Her heart was pounding like a drum, her breath roared in her own ears. Suddenly she saw a broken chair leg on the floor nearby and snatched it up.

She whirled, but she was too late. He was already upon her.

Thick fingers were pressing her throat. Bright lights began to burst in her brain like fireworks.

She struggled frantically, beating her hands against that awful face, but instead of the grip on her throat slackening, the fierce pressure increased, and the sharp, needlelike pains behind her eyes became white hot . . .

Chapter Fourteen

The man known as Miguel was dark and slim. He had narrow shoulders and hooded, deep-set eyes punched into a narrow pockmarked face. He wore long black sideburns and a pencil-thin mustache. His glistening white teeth were clamped around a black cheroot.

With his tightly waisted jacket, vividly striped shirt and pinstriped trousers, he reminded Steve Martin of a mobster of the Roaring Twenties. His jet black hair was sleeked down until it shone, and he stank of cologne—the best. Everything about Miguel was expensive: the suit, the cheroot, the shoes, the diamond-studded gold lighter.

Miguel had been born in an adobe hut in a squalid, stinking Mexican village. There had never been any extra money—ever. And now that there was, he spent it ostentatiously, revealing his insecurity. His family, still alive, were of course forgotten. They continued to live in filthy surroundings, in abject poverty, while his current mistress occupied a penthouse and spent more in a week on cosmetics than Miguel's family had to exist on for a year. When Miguel thought about them, which wasn't often, he was amused.

Behind Miguel stood Vorrelli. He was wearing his black-rimmed sunglasses. He peered down at Steve, who was bound to a wooden-backed bedroom chair.

"It's the guy who was on the plane coming over," he said. "He's been seeing the doll."

"Where's he staying?"

"The Continentale."

"Know anything about him?"

"He's a writer, so he says, doing research on the chateau. Name's Steve Martin."

"He's the first writer I've met who carried a gun."

"It's as well you arrived when you did," Vorrelli said. "Maybe it was him who killed Max."

Miguel's cold, snakelike eyes bored down into Steve's. "Did you?" he asked. There was evil in those eyes; they were evil and repellent. He was a man who would show no mercy.

"Who the devil is Max?" asked Steve.

"He worked for me," said Vorrelli, tonelessly. "Right now he's lying under a pile of rubble in the old wing of the chateau—as though you didn't know."

"Not guilty," grunted Steve. "Why would I want to kill him? And would someone like to give me a smoke?"

Miguel lit a cigarette and stuffed it between Steve's lips.

"Thanks. I didn't know there was a way into that part of the chateau anyway . . . I wish I did."

Vorrelli frowned. "You interested in the Duvals —or the girl?"

"The girl—Ann Preston. I'm worried about her."

"Worried?"

"I don't like the rumors I've heard in the village. The Duvals are a crazy bunch, and the chateau is said to be haunted. I don't like the idea of her living there."

"That doesn't explain what you were doing here," said Vorrelli.

"I heard you were on the scene when her car crashed—and I know someone tampered with the brakes. I had an idea you might be responsible; otherwise, why did you take off when the police arrived? I wanted to know what was behind it."

"A hero," sneered Miguel. He leaned forward and struck Steve a stinging blow that made his head sing. "Now tell us the *real* reason you were snooping around here?"

"I've told you!" Steve snapped. His lip was

split by the blow, and blood trickled down his chin.

"And it smells! Ever heard of Big French?"

"No."

"What part of the States you from?"

"New York—but I've been in Denmark for the past three years."

"He could be telling the truth," Vorrelli muttered.

"If you believe that, you'll believe anything," the Mexican jeered.

Vorrelli stiffened. "Don't talk that way to me! Anyway, what does it matter who he is right now. There's more important things to do."

"Such as?"

"The doll. The Duvals have tried to kill her once, they'll try again. This time they might be successful. We've got to get her first. Now!"

Miguel said, "Okay, you're the big wheel." He jerked his head in Steve's direction. "What do we do about *him?*"

Vorrelli stroked his beard. He glanced toward the window. "There's a small craft in the shed adjoining the villa. When it gets dark, you take him out to sea and dump him over the side. Maybe the fish 'll like him better than I do. Meanwhile, gag him, and let's get going."

When the door closed behind them Steve started straining against the ropes binding his wrist. But they had been tied by an expert; he could try for hours and never succeed in loosening them. Somehow he had to get free—not only to save his own life, but to save Ann! Whatever plan the two men had in mind, he knew that it boded Ann no good.

He heard the front door slam and the sounds of hurrying footsteps on the shingle outside. A car door banged shut, and the engine roared.

It was vital that he free himself somehow and get to Ann before Vorrelli and Miguel did. Failure meant that not only would he be killed, but Ann would die also.

He tensed, trying to jerk the chair and himself toward the window. The chair rocked; he steadied himself. If he crashed to the floor he might not be able to heave himself up right again.

It was a slow, bone-jarring task. He moved an inch at a time. His legs and arms ached, and the gag almost choked him. Sweat streamed down his forehead, but, inch by inch, he edged closer to the window. It was dusk now, and shadows were lengthening across the room; outside the sky was leaden as though there were a storm in the air.

Another two feet . . .

Even then it wouldn't be easy. Once next to the window he somehow had to smash one of the panes and hope that a fragment would fall to the floor where he could reach it. After that it meant he would have to tip the chair over enough to pick up the piece of glass.

The room was much darker now. For hours—he had lost count of time, but it must have been more than twenty hours since Miguel had surprised him the previous night—he had sat bound in the hard chair. Every muscle ached and screamed for relief.

A black storm cloud hovered in the sky. Soon lightning forked and was followed almost immediately by the deep rumble of thunder. A few spots of rain spattered against the windowpane.

How long had the two men been gone?

Fifteen—twenty minutes? He didn't know; but they must be nearing the chateau by this time.

Swearing, sweating, he heaved the chair forward again, but overbalanced. He crashed heavily to the floor, the chair on top of him. He lay there cursing, wondering what the hell he was going to do.

His whole body pained him; his legs felt drained of all strength. A draft beneath the bedroom door whispered against his ears. He had failed. He would have to lie there until they returned with Ann. They would laugh at him, jeer, probably kick him around.

They would question Ann, then put on the pressure. What they would do would be unpleasant. They had learned from the Gestapo—and Miguel would probably add his own refinements.

And she wouldn't talk—not because of courage, or because it was vital that she shouldn't—but simply because she didn't know what it was they wanted from her. She had no idea at all what it was all about. He hadn't known the full score himself until the arrival of that cable. His only interest until then had been to discover if Vorrelli had located Big French's money.

And when they'd finished with Ann they would do to her what they proposed doing to him: take her out in a boat and dump her into the sea.

The thought gave him new fear . . . and new strength. He tried once more to heave himself upright, but he was merely wasting his time and knew it. Drenched with sweat he relaxed his aching, protesting muscles. Give up and conserve your strength, he told himself. Maybe you'll get an opportunity later. They'll have to cut you free when the time comes to take you aboard the boat.

Then he froze.

Someone was tapping against the window!

He looked up, renewed hope in his heart. There was a face at the window—that of Tom Langognes! He was pointing into the villa, looking at Steven inquiringly. The gesture was obvious.

Eagerly, Steve shook his head vigorously from side to side, and the face disappeared.

Moments later Tom was removing the gag and slashing through the cords which bound Steve to the chair.

"I've never been more pleased to see anyone in my life!" Steve confessed as he massaged his wrists. "How the devil did you get on to me?"

"I phoned the estate agents in Biarritz. I described the man with the beard, and they gave me this address. I was sure you were here when I found your car parked in the field up the lane."

Steve was struggling from the last of his ropes, stamping his feet, and swinging his arms to restore the circulation. Then he began to hobble toward the door.

"There's no time to lose," he said. "Those two devils have gone to get Ann. We've got to reach her before they do!"

Chapter Fifteen

For Pierre Duval it had been a day of changing moods of elation and severe depression, and he knew only too well that these signs heralded another attack.

First would come the dull ache in his head which would grow increasingly worse as though his skull had become encircled by a shrinking steel band. The drumming in his head would become deafening, and he would be possessed by an overpowering desire for release at any cost.

His mind would retreat from reality and become filled with vivid pictures, dredged up from his subconscious. He would see the old familiar circus ring again, the gleaming trapezes, the blurred, upturned faces of the audience below. He would hear the soft music, would smell the odor of expectancy rising from below, mingled with the smell of peeled oranges and animal sweat.

Every eye would be focused on him. The shuffling of feet, the cracking of peanut shells would cease, and everyone would be still. No more toffee papers would be folded in strips between nervous fingers; no more crackling of chocolate wrappers, just complete and utter silence as he swung backward and forward on the trapeze with ever increasing speed.

Later he would slither down the rope hanging beside the gently swaying trapeze. He would switch off the arc lights, the spinning recorder spools, change out of the spangled tights—and he would feel exhilarated, the dreadful pressures gone, the screaming nerves relaxed.

At first, when these attacks had begun, Juliette had been frightened. She had said that he would kill himself, but when she realized that he did himself no harm and had been quick to perceive a change in him—the moodiness and irritability gone—she accepted his condition. On occasions she even encouraged him, knowing it would make him feel better.

But these past few days she had been awkward he thought peevishly. It was her age, he supposed . . . and how quickly she was aging!

"You must control yourself, at least for the time being," she had told him sharply. "I want Ann to stay here."

"But I can't help having these attacks!" he protested. "And Ann doesn't mind. Why, last time she applauded me!"

"Perhaps. But you frightened her, nevertheless. Another time she might feel differently. I don't want her scared away."

"She's a sweet girl," he said. "She isn't frightened of me. A pity our Yvette is not more like her."

"Don't change the subject, Pierre. You will put your lamps and your equipment away. It won't be for always. Just as soon as the work is completed and she has gone, you may erect them again in the library."

But for once Pierre was determined to have his own way. It was ridiculous! Why should a pretty, intelligent girl be frightened by a trapeze artist! And a star at that!

She was, he reflected irritably, far more likely to be driven away by that slimy reptile his wife kept in the big wicker basket in the overheated lounge. The woman had no sense—or she was both selfish and stupid.

But as usual he had not argued. He had meekly taken down the arc lights, the electrical cables, and the trapezes and carried them out of the library.

The days that followed had been exciting, he thought gleefully as he made his way along the dark upstairs corridor. Oh, beautifully exciting!

He used to sit at the end of the dining table and watch her, hugging his secret to him. If only she knew. If only she knew.

But Juliette didn't know; she hadn't even the slightest suspicion.

It hadn't been too difficult to make the necessary electrical connections in the west wing. He'd secretly bought the necessary plugs, the extra cable and insulating tape. Today he knew that an attack was imminent; and hurriedly changing he now sped along the dark twisting corridors, his eyes bright with expectancy and triumph.

And then, as he padded out onto the minstrel's gallery, he heard Ann scream. . . .

The shrill, terrifying sound came from the gloomy hall below. For a moment Pierre Duval stood completely still, startled almost completely back to reality. The cries came again, penetrating the gray mist that swirled and eddied in his brain.

"Help! Help!"

There was something vaguely familiar about the voice. He screwed up his eyes, trying to place it. It belonged to someone he knew, someone he liked . . .

Then, in a blinding flash of illumination, he realized who was screaming. It was Ann, of course. Ann, the English girl—the girl who had applauded his act on the trapeze. Who had told him that she had never witnessed a performance like it, anywhere.

He leapt towards one of the massive, ornately decorated pillars which supported the roof of the gallery. His hands closed over the electric light switch he had recently screwed there. Just for a second he felt a slight tremor of current through his fingers. Then he pressed down the switch.

One moment the great hall was in darkness, lit only by the pale light that filtered through the hole in the tiles at the far end.

The next moment it was as bright as day. Arc lamps blazed down from the ceiling; the damp, crumbling walls, the disorder of broken chairs, the suspended trapezes, the puddles reflecting the light—all sprang vividly to sight.

Then he saw Ann beating at the man who was bending over her, his hands at her throat, oblivious it seemed of the blinding light.

Pierre Duval did not hesitate.

He sprang to the balustrade of the gallery with remarkable agility. For a moment he poised there, then he launched himself forward, his hands outstretched. He hurtled toward the steel bar of the nearest trapeze. His hands closed about it, the momentum sending him forward at speed. His legs jackknifed, and the trapeze swung back, gathered more speed, sped forward again.

Now his feet were clamped together, his legs

rigid. His eyes were gleaming, and his body was tensed. He released his hold on the steel bar and shot forward like a bullet from a gun.

Seconds later his feet struck the crouched man heavily in the back of the neck with terrific force. There was a crack like the snapping of a twig. The man stumbled forward and crashed headfirst into a pile of broken chairs, scattering them. Then he tumbled to the floor and lay still.

Duval had landed like a cat. He jumped up and ran to Ann's side; he knelt down beside her. Her face was pale, her eyes closed, and she was breathing laboriously. There were ugly red marks on her throat, but he saw that she was still alive.

He raised his eyes and stared toward the sprawled figure of her attacker. There was puzzlement on his childlike face. Something about the man struck a familiar chord in his mind. He moved over to him and turned him over. Horror sprang to his eyes as he gazed down at the scarred and distorted face.

"*Mon Dieu!*" he whispered brokenly.

For one shocked and horrified moment he continued to stare down at the dead man, then he turned away.

"Oh, poor Ann!" he said softly. "What a terrible, terrible thing to happen to her."

Gently he lifted the unconscious girl in his arms and carried her up the wide staircase to the gallery.

He moved swiftly along the dark, disused corridors as though she was light as a feather. Within a minute or two he had lowered her on to her own bed in her own room and hurried downstairs.

He went straight to the library and lifted the receiver. To his relief the line had been repaired, and he spoke quickly. Then he summoned Marie and instructed her to go to Ann's room.

"There has been an accident," he said. "Stay with her until the doctor arrives. Tell her when she comes round that I have sent for him and that she has nothing to fear now. Go quickly!"

As the white-faced maid ran up the stairs, Duval entered the second-floor lounge. Juliette was sitting by the fire, crooning to the snake which was coiled on her lap. Her eyes snapped at sight of the little man in his spangled tights.

"What are you doing dressed like that? I thought I told you—" Her voice broke off. He faced her unsmiling, his eyes hard. She sensed a new authority in him—a terrible anger.

"What is the matter, Pierre? Why are you looking at me like that?"

"Put that wretched thing down and listen to me!"

She was startled at the tone of command in his voice and obeyed, letting the python drop to the floor at her side. She was puzzled now, even a little afraid. She had never known him to be like this before.

"What is it, my Pierre?"

"Why didn't you tell me?"

"Tell you? Tell you what?"

"That Gaston—was here," he said slowly. "That Gaston was—alive."

She caught her breath. "You've seen him?"

"I have seen him." He closed his eyes and ran a trembling hand through his hair. "His face," he muttered. "Oh, his poor face . . ."

"I did not want to upset you, Pierre," she whimpered. "I knew that sight of him would do terrible things to you. He—he is not well since those devils tortured him. Like you, I believed that he was dead, but he escaped—after they had tortured him. Then he was—he was involved in a—a car accident and hopelessly disfigured, as you saw. He was hidden by simple folk who took pity on him. He was broken in mind and body, and many months later, while you were in Paris, I had him brought here. He has been here ever since. I couldn't have him put in a mental home. How could I? My son—*our* son. . . ."

"It was Gaston who attacked that girl from the village?" said Pierre quietly. "Of course. I saw the photograph in the newspaper. She looked like Denise, the girl who betrayed him, the girl he loved.

But why Ann? She has never done him any harm."

The woman's voice sharpened. "Ann?" she queried.

"He just attacked her—in the west wing."

Something almost resembling a smile crossed her lined, yellowed face. "She is dead?" There was no emotion in her voice.

He shook his head. "No, thank God. I got to her in time. It is—Gaston who is dead."

"Gaston? Dead!" She had risen, her face was parchment white now where it had been yellow, her dark eyes sunken and staring. "No, Pierre, it is not true! It is some joke you are playing to punish me!"

"No, Juliette. It is true."

"I will not believe it!" Her voice rose to a shrill scream. "It is not true! I will *not* believe it!"

"I did not mean to do it," said Pierre sadly. "I jumped on him from the trapeze . . . it broke his neck, I think. I only did it to stop him from killing Ann."

Something in Juliette snapped. She towered over him like a demented Amazon, her hands clawing at his face, her mouth wide open in a soundless scream, her hair tumbling about her lined and hollowed cheeks.

"You fool! You murderer!" she screamed. "You have killed him! You have killed Gaston, my son."

Sobbing hysterically, forgetting the stick which

lay unheeded on the floor, she went limping and hobbling from the room.

Dusk was creeping over the chateau. The doctor had come and gone, had said that apart from a sore throat Ann would be practically recovered by morning. He had given her a sedative, and she had spent the rest of the day in a restful slumber.

Juliette had gone to her room. The doctor had tried to give her a sedative also, but she had refused it. She had locked her door and refused to come out, in spite of Pierre's pleas.

Now she opened the door to allow Yvette to enter, quickly closing and locking it again.

"You can't blame papa," Yvette muttered as she sat on the bed and watched her mother limp restlessly around the bedroom. "How was he to know that Gaston was alive? Like everybody else, he believed that he was dead."

Juliette raised eyes from which all hope and understanding had gone; they were as glazed and unseeing as the eyes of the python in its wicker basket.

"Nothing you can say will bring Gaston back," she said bitterly. "To think that he should have died thus—after all that he has suffered through. And all because of that wretched, hateful girl!"

"Perhaps it was retribution," said Yvette.

"What do you mean?"

"I don't have to spell it out, do I? How can you try to make out that it was her fault. If she hadn't been attacked—if you hadn't insisted on living in your stupid dream-world instead of having Gaston put away—it would never have happened." She shivered. "I don't mind telling you, I haven't felt safe in bed at night, knowing that he was prowling around in the old wing, avenging himself on everybody he could lay his hands on! That girl from the village . . ."

"He was sick. He had suffered so. How he had suffered, my poor Gaston! First Denise whom he loved, and who betrayed him; then all that he underwent after he was captured. You will come qirh me to look at his body, Yvette? I have had him taken to his old room . . ."

Yvette shivered. "No. I would sooner remember him as he was, not as he is now."

"As you wish," Juliette said coldly. "But he was your brother—your only brother. But then, you never loved him, did you? You never loved anyone but yourself—"

"Oh, for God's sake, don't go on so!" said Yvette.

"She shall pay," Juliette said, her mouth grimly set, her hand quivering on the silver-tipped stick. "More than ever now, she shall pay!"

Her eyes were suddenly blazing, and the viciousness in her voice sent a cold icy finger tracing down Yvette's spine. No wonder she was what she was, Yvette thought despairingly, with a mother like this.

She said, "You're crazy, mama. As crazy as Gaston was! The police aren't fools. There has been talk in the village about the car brakes being tampered with; if Ann tells of the launch sinking—"

"It has to be done! That's all there is to it," said the woman angrily. "There will be no danger for anyone, and you will benefit. With her dead, your American friend will turn to you for comfort—if you have sense enough to play your cards right. That is what you want, isn't it?"

"I'm not sure that I do," Yvette muttered. "Not this way. Perhaps I'm growing up—at last. Maybe that's what love does to you."

"Love! What do you know about love? Young people these days know nothing of love—only sex. I cannot keep pace with the ideas of your generation, and your so-called permissive society."

"No, because you're so obsessed with your own ideas that you haven't time for anything else."

Her mother's eyes flashed. "Leave me alone! You know how I hate you smoking in my room! It is a disgusting habit. There should be a law against it."

As Yvette got up from the bed and stamped out, Juliette crossed to the window and stood staring out across the grounds, a tear coursing down her lined cheeks.

But the resolution in her mind was unshaken. Ann had to die. And this time the attempt *must* succeed—before she had a chance to leave the chateau. Juliette had a feeling that even if Gaston had not attacked Ann when he did, the girl had already made plans to return to her friends. First the accident with the car, then the sinking of the launch. She would be a fool if she did not suspect something!

The arrival and departure of the doctor had sown in Juliette's mind the seeds of an idea. He had left behind a small bottle of sleeping tablets on the small table beside Ann's bed. It would be a simple enough matter to give her an overdose in a glass of hot milk.

The police would think that, in her dazed and drugged condition, the girl had inadvertently taken too many pills.

Certainly they would not be able to prove otherwise.

Chapter Sixteen

Yvette knew that, more than anything else in the world, she wanted Steve Martin to love her.

He was the kind of man she had always dreamed about, a man almost physically the twin of the current Parisian idol of her own fickle generation. There had been minor, unimportant affairs in Paris, which at the time she had believed to be the "real thing." But with conquest had come disillusion. This time she knew it was real.

There had been no one in her life like him, and she felt sure that there never would be again. It wasn't only his physical appearance which attracted her; she sensed in him a personal integrity which she had never experienced before. If her mother carried out her plan to remove Ann, then there would be no further opposition. He would be upset, naturally, but after all he hadn't known her that long. And she, Yvette, would be there, close at hand; the willing companion, understanding and sympathetic always.

But—was Ann's death the only way in which she could get Steve? Wouldn't it be on her conscience for the rest of her life? When she had first heard of her mother's plan she had been frightened. Her first impulse had been to appeal to her father; but Juliette dominated him so completely that she knew he would be powerless. She couldn't go to the police; to do so would be to incriminate her father also. And in spite of everything, she could not forget the kindness and the affection he had shown to her as a child. She couldn't betray him.

But would Juliette go through with it, now that Gaston was dead? Did she care enough now?

These conflicting thoughts filled her mind as she got to her feet and went slowly upstairs to Ann's room.

"Oh, m'amselle!" Marie exclaimed as Yvette opened the door. "How you startle me!"

"I'm sorry, Marie. You may go for a cup of coffee now. I'll sit with Ann for a while."

The girl shot Yvette a quick uneasy glance. But Ann, lying back against the pillow, conscious now, gave Yvette a smile.

"It's all right, Marie," she said reassuringly. "I feel much better now. I'll be quite all right. And thank you very much for sitting with me all this time."

The maid went out, and Yvette sat down in the chair nearest Ann's bed. The room was illuminated only by the bedside lamp.

"I thought I'd look in," she said. "How are you feeling now?"

"Much better," said Ann. Her hands strayed unconsciously to the bandage about her throat and, against her will, she gave a sudden convulsive shudder. The sedative had helped dispel some of the horror of the attack, but it was still fresh in her mind. That horrible fact, those tight-gripping hands . . .

She said, "I'm sorry about your brother, Yvette. Marie told me."

Yvette's eyes suddenly filled with tears. She said, with a certain viciousness, "Oh, why do you have to be so . . . so damned *nice* all the time! Gaston nearly strangles you—and all you can say is that you're sorry—for him!" She added, "Anyway, I don't deserve that you should be nice to me. I've been pretty rotten to you."

"Because of Steve?"

"I suppose so. We'd probably have got on famously together if it hadn't been for him . . . if he hadn't fallen in love with you. It's pretty grim being stuck in this beastly place all the time, with a couple of nut cases!"

Ann hid a smile. "You shouldn't talk that way, Yvette. They are your parents, after all. And they're certainly not 'nut cases.' Your father may be—eccentric, but after all he did save my life. And your mother—"

"Oh, don't make excuses for mama. She's properly out of her mind," said Yvette calmly. "I mean, letting everyone think Gaston was dead, and keeping him here secretly all that time. Knowing he was mentally ill—dangerous . . ."

"Did you know?"

"Not at first. I found out quite by accident. I was shocked at first, then I thought: what the hell if it amuses her to keep him around. I'm rarely at home anyway. And she's always been completely obsessed by Gaston . . . she never did have time for me. All she ever lived for was Gaston, Gaston, Gaston!" The girl's voice was bitter.

Yvette stopped speaking and looked at Ann. Then she said, "But I didn't come here to talk about my brother. I came to warn you. You can't stay here any longer—it's too dangerous."

"I know," said Ann soberly. "They've been trying to kill me, haven't they? At least, I think your mother has."

Yvette stared at her in amazement. "You *knew?*"

"I'd be a fool not to suspect, wouldn't I? The

tampering with the brakes, the sinking of the launch. . . . Do you know *why?*"

Yvette flushed. "I can't tell you. But you must get up now, this minute. Slip away from the house. My mother is up to something. I don't know what she's got in mind, but I do know that you're in danger. Come on, I'll help you."

"But . . . but I thought you didn't like me!" Ann stammered.

"I don't—but I draw the line at murder," said Yvette, flinching inwardly as she realized how near she had come to condoning it. It was as though blindness had been lifted from her eyes, and she could see clearly for the first time.

Yvette picked up Ann's suitcase, snapped it open, and began to cram the contents of the dressing-table drawers into it. "For heaven's sake, hurry!" she flung at Ann. "Mama might come in at any moment. I don't know what she means to do—but she's crazy enough for anything. She might try to keep you here by force."

Ann quickly scrambled into her clothes and pulled on her shoes. She cast a quick glance around the room as Yvette, carrying Ann's case, opened the door and peered along the gloomy corridor. Ann wouldn't be at all sorry to leave this chateau and the people in it, although she would have liked to see Pierre Duval and thank him for saving her life. It seemed ungracious to slip away without a word to him—especially since he had killed his own son to save her.

"Hurry, damn you!" said Yvette. "I can hear someone coming."

To Ann's surprise, the girl turned toward the west wing. Ann shivered, feeling a moment's dread as the memory of that terrible scene flashed in front of her eyes again. Would she ever forget it? For a split second she hesitated. Could she really trust Yvette? Had the girl been telling the truth—or was she lying for her own ends? After all, she was in love with Steve, and she had once told Ann that she would do anything to get—and keep—him.

If Yvette was harboring thoughts of treachery toward her, what better place to put them into action but in the west wing? Ann still felt hazy from the effects of the sleeping pill; she knew that if it came to a physical showdown she would be no match for the agile French girl. She only needed a quick push as they crossed the gaping floorboards, and there would be another 'accident.' This time a fatal one.

"Come quickly I tell you!" Yvette's voice broke in on her thoughts. The girl's voice held a faint note of hysteria as well as impatience.

Ann looked at her; her head was beginning to swim; her legs felt curiously weak. She felt the other girl's hand as it closed upon her arm and gave a little tug. Reluctantly she allowed herself to be led along the dark corridor, past Raymonde's room and into the west wing.

Her heart was hammering wildly, and she could hardly control her fear.

Was Yvette leading her into a trap? Anything could happen here, in the darkness, amongst these desolate surroundings.

She opened her handbag, took a small flashlight from it. She pulled herself free of Yvette's clutching fingers, hung back a little. If the other girl really intended to attack her, then she would be ready.

"Hurry up!" called Yvette. "What's the matter with you?"

Ann said breathlessly, "You're not going through that hall where Gaston—"

"No, there's a quicker way. At the end of this corridor there's a door leading to a staircase which goes down to the basement. We can go through the servants' old quarters, through the cellars and out onto the grounds." Her mood seemed to have changed; she gave a little jeering laugh. "Getting scared? Afraid I might be going to try something?"

"Of course not," Ann lied.

"I wouldn't blame you if you were, after all that's happened to you here." She paused. "This is the door, I think. I haven't been here since I was a child."

She stiffened. A long, shrill, piercing scream had come suddenly from behind them.

"*What*—" Yvette turned, her face going suddenly white.

"It's your mother!" gasped Ann. "She must have been following us. She's met with an accident or something . . . we must go back!"

It did not matter that Juliette had tried to kill her, that she was probably in the very act of making a third attempt. The Frenchwoman had been hurt, and Ann could not leave her there in the darkness, perhaps in pain.

The two girls cautiously retraced their steps, edging around the ragged holes in the floorboards, guided by the beam from the light Yvette was carrying. Filmy cobwebs brushed Ann's face like spidery fingers. They came at last to a landing, and a sudden gasp burst from Ann's lips.

Ahead of them the rotting floorboards had collapsed and plunged down into the cellars beneath. She edged forward carefully, and Yvette shone the powerful beam downward.

Some twenty feet below them Juliette Duval lay spread-eagled on the floor. Her silver-tipped stick lay close by. She was lying on her face, her neck was twisted awkwardly. Some of the old flooring lay across her back.

"Oh my God!" muttered Yvette.

Ann shook off her feeling of horror and looked

around her. "She may still be alive. We've got to get to her. Is there a way from here." She shook the French girl who seemed paralyzed from shock. "Yvette! Pull yourself together! We must help your mother!"

Yvette stared at her dazedly. "Yes, yes, I'll show you." There was a sob in her voice as she led the way into one of the rooms.

Ann saw a narrow, winding staircase in the corner, leading down. A few minutes later she found herself kneeling beside Juliette Duval's body.

Blood was trickling from the corner of her mouth, and an ugly bruise was already forming down one side of her face, from the temple to the line of her jaw. One glance told Ann that there was nothing she could do, nothing that anyone could do now.

"I'm afraid she's dead," she told Yvette gently.

"You're sure? You're quite sure?"

"Yes. We'd better send for the doctor again. How do we get back from here?"

Her eyes moist, Yvette stared down at the crumpled figure of her mother. "We never got on well," she said. "But she was my mother. Oh, what made me like I was?"

"Don't," said Ann gently. "We'd better get back to the house. There's no point in my leaving now."

They crossed the cellar. It was then that the two

men came from behind the stacked furniture in the corner.

"No, baby, this way."

Ann swung round in alarm, levelling her own light, shining the thin beam at the voice.

The voice snarled, "Keep that light down, damn you!"

A strong beam of light blinded her as she automatically lowered her own, but not before she had recognized the bearded man. Behind him was a thinner, darker figure with a gun in his hand. He gestured with the weapon.

"This way."

"But my mother!" wailed Yvette.

"She's not going anywhere," Vorrelli said callously.

Fear stirred in the pit of Ann's stomach as she walked through the cellar door. Yvette was crying softly. Ann slipped her arm around the girl's waist and picked her way through the heap of rubble and broken furniture.

The sour smell of decay was everywhere; it filled her lungs and made her feel sick.

At last she crawled through the hole in the wall and out into the cold night air, with Yvette at her heels. The prickly bushes tore at her stockings, but she was barely conscious of them. What was it all about? Who were these men and what did they want of her? Did they really believe that she knew where the "loot" was hidden—wherever that might be?

"This way!" The thinner man with the gun dug her brutally in the ribs. He thrust her forward through the dark, overgrown bushes of the garden. The sky was cloud filled; away at sea lightning flashed in long ragged streaks. A violent crack of thunder made her jump, then rain started to fall.

Ann and Yvette were pushed along the narrow path which encircled the old chateau. To Ann's surprise they knocked at the front door, and when it was opened by the startled Raymonde, they pushed him back inside, stepping quickly into the hall.

"Don't try any tricks, and you won't get hurt," grunted Vorrelli. "Where's Duval?"

The gaunt-faced butler had been taken completely by surprise. All his assurance seemed to leave him. "Upstairs," he stammered unhappily.

"Take us!"

Pierre Duval was standing with his back to the fireplace as they entered the lounge, Ann and Yvette side by side, the looming figures of the two men behind them. He blinked in astonishment.

"What is the meaning of this?" he demanded.

"Sit down!" snarled Miguel. "And keep your lips buttoned."

"Now, Miss Preston," said Vorrelli softly. "You know why we're here. Where is it? You can save yourself a lot of grief if you talk now." He jerked his head toward the Mexican and smiled coldly. "This is my friend, Miguel, the one I was telling you about, the guy with the persuasive methods!"

Ann said, "I tell you: I know *nothing* about any money!"

"Next you'll say that the name of Henri Duval means nothing to you, that you didn't know he was Big French!"

Yvette gasped. "Uncle Henri!"

"That's right, honey."

Pierre was staring in bewilderment, his childlike face screwed up in perplexity. "My brother, Henri—" he began.

"Shut up, you!" said Vorrelli savagely. "Well, Miss Preston?"

"I've never met him." Ann was completely bewildered. "I've never even *heard* of him!"

"Yeah?" sneered Miguel. "Then how come he left this dump to you?"

Ann stared incredulously. She was so astounded that she could hardly speak. When she did her voice cracked.

"Left me—the chateau?" she repeated.

"Everything, and don't play the innocent with me!"

"But—but you *must* be mistaken!" Ann gasped. Her brain was reeling. The old chateau—hers? Was this the reason Juliette has tried to kill her?

Was it because she had loved the old ruined house which had sheltered both her and her beloved Gaston for so long? "I—I—don't understand," she said feebly.

Vorrelli was beginning to look uneasy. He wondered if there had been a mistake; surely nobody who looked so completely confused and disbelieving could be lying?

"Lies!" snarled Miguel suddenly. His voice was harsh. "Listen: Big French was a mobster. One of the most powerful in the States. He had a finger in every pie: cathouses, protection, international secrets for sale. You name it, Big French was behind it. A week ago he was gunned down, in Washington—maybe by the commies he was trying to doublecross."

"But—" began Ann.

"He was planning to retire, to come back here. He wanted out. He'd salted plenty away; much of it was smuggled out and brought over here. You inherit the whole estate, so you must know where the loot's hidden."

"But I don't!" cried Ann. "I thought the chateau belonged to Monsieur Duval. I came here to work as his secretary. I don't know anything about—about Big French—or his money! I've never even heard of him, I tell you!"

She broke off, her eyes widening in horror. She tried to shout a warning, but no sound came. She stared agape, her eyes protruding from her head, at what she could see undulating along the blackened beam above Vorrelli's head.

The next instant it had slithered down and dropped around the American's shoulders.

He screamed. His glassy eyes bulged in panic. The writhing, rippling body was coiling itself about his body, squeezing, squeezing. He could feel his ribs beginning to crack under the pressure, feel the air being forced from his lungs.

"Do something!" he screamed. "For God's sake, do something!"

Miguel had raised the gun, then lowered it. He could not fire at the snake without hitting Vorrelli. Yvette and Ann stood there, paralyzed with horror, all color drained from their faces. Duval sat transfixed, sweating from every pore. Nobody could move; it was like a tableau seen through a block of ice.

Then it was all over. The snake began slowly to uncoil itself, began to slither across the floor, and the pudgy figure of Vorrelli dropped like a rag doll.

Only then did Miguel come to his senses. He fired twice, shattering the snake's poised head. Suddenly, behind him, other forms appeared in the open doorway.

Ann glanced up; for an instant her heart seemed to stand still from joy and relief. Steve Martin and

Tom Langognes had seemingly materialized out of nowhere—and Steve had a gun levelled at the slim figure of the Mexican.

"Drop it!" he snapped.

With a snarl of fury Miguel snapped off two more shots. A splinter of wood flew from the door jamb, less than two inches from Steve's face. Steve fired and missed; his shot shattered a window into a hundred tinkling fragments. The reports echoed deafeningly in the lofty hall.

He fired again.

Miguel had wrenched open a door and leapt through it. He was still in midleap when Steve's second bullet struck him. He staggered, fell to his knees, turned. With his last spasmodic effort he raised the gun and fired again.

On the other side of the room Pierre Duval gave a sudden gasp. He jerked under the impact of the bullet, then fell forward, tumbling from his chair like a disjointed marionette; he was killed instantly.

It was two hours later, and Steve and Ann were seated in Peggy's lounge; Tom and Yvette were still at the chateau. When everything was cleared up, Tom had told Steve he would be going with Yvette to Paris. He felt that, with both her parents dead, she would need somebody to look after her.

Ann said, "What I still can't understand, Steve, is why the chateau was left to *me*. I've never had any connection at all with the Duval family."

Steve grinned at her, placing his hand warmly upon hers.

"I don't know the full details myself—yet," he said. "But it seems that Henri Duval knew your father. They were on safari once, and your father saved his life when a wounded lion attacked. Henri never forgot. He lived in a world where it was every man for himself; nobody else he knew would have risked their own life to save him. Your father was hurt, too—pretty badly; Henri never forgot that either.

"He made a will leaving everything to your father. When your father died you, as his only relative naturally inherited. Only after your death would the estate revert to the Duval family, but to Pierre. Henri had never liked Juliette, whom he considered mean and grasping. He had no great love for Pierre, either, but he didn't mind them living at the chateau while he was in the States."

Ann snuggled down in the chair closer to Steve. "But how are you involved, Steve?" she asked.

He removed his hand from hers, put his arm around her shoulders.

"Me? I guess I'm just a government man of no importance. Before Big French died, we'd heard a rumor that he was stashing away his loot over here. When he died my job was to watch Vorrelli, one of his lieutenants. We figured he would know where it was hidden and come after it. It wasn't until later that I learned you were, in fact, heiress to the estate. I bribed Raymonde to keep an eye on you—though I must confess I didn't think at first that Juliette would try to kill you. But when I heard about the brakes having been tampered with I knew you were in the gravest danger."

"Do you think the money will be found?" asked Ann.

He shrugged. "We'll probably find a lead when we go through Big French's papers. I'd like to stick around and help you, if I may."

"There's nothing I'd like more, Steve," she said. "I'll let Yvette use the chateau for as long as she likes. She has no real home now, you know, and no parents either. She's quite alone, except for—"

"Except for Tom," he said.

"Do you think . . ." Ann did not finish the sentence, but he knew what she meant, and he nodded reassuringly.

"Perhaps. She's a different girl now. I think she'll find that Tom is the kind of man she really needs. At first I think he felt sorry for her, but I believe it may go deeper than that. Anyway, we'll hope for the best, shall we?"

Ann said, "Pierre was always very kind to me. I can't believe he had anything to do with—with Juliette's plans to kill me. At any rate, I would like to think that he didn't. I can't help feeling sad about his death."

"Perhaps it was for the best," said Steve somberly. "Without Juliette he would have been completely helpless. He depended on her in so many ways. And of course, those attacks he had—in spite of what he or she told you—were undoubtedly growing more frequent. In the end, they might have lead him to the asylum. Better death than a madhouse."

"I suppose you're right," she agreed unhappily. Suddenly a thought struck her and she smiled. "About the chateau . . ." she said. "Yvette's always hated it; perhaps she'll want to stay in Paris. . . . How would *you* like to live there?"

He stared at her. "Me?"

"Us then," she said. She looked at him mischievously. "In case you've forgotten, it's Leap Year, and I'm proposing to you. And if you should decide to accept—"

"If?" he repeated, his arm tightening about her shoulders, his eyes glowing with renewed warmth. "Why you know darned well there's no if about it."

"As I just said," she continued demurely, "if you decide to accept me, after we're married you can write your book at the chateau." She broke off, for he was pulling her toward him and his mouth was very close to her own.

"After we're married, who the hell wants to waste time writing books?" he demanded as he kissed her.

And not even Ann could find an answer to that.

LOOK FOR OUR MAGNUM CLASSICS

ADVENTURES OF PINOCCHIO by Carlo Collodi
AESOP'S FABLES by Aesop
ALICE'S ADVENTURES IN WONDERLAND &
  THROUGH THE LOOKING GLASS by Lewis Carroll
AROUND THE WORLD IN 80 DAYS by Jules Verne
AUTOBIOGRAPHY OF BENJAMIN FRANKLIN
  by Benjamin Franklin
BLACK BEAUTY by Anna Sewell
CALL OF THE WILD by Jack London
"CAPTAIN COURAGEOUS" by Rudyard Kipling
CHRISTMAS CAROL by Charles Dickens
EREWHON by Samuel Butler
FIRST MEN IN THE MOON by H. G. Wells
FRANKENSTEIN by Mary Shelley
GREEN MANSIONS by W. H. Hudson
HAMLET by William Shakespeare
HANS BRINKER: OR, THE SILVER SKATES
  by Mary Mapes Dodge
HEIDI by Johana Spyri
HOUND OF THE BASKERVILLES by A. Conan Doyle
INVISIBLE MAN by H. G. Wells
ISLAND OF DR. MOREAU by H. G. Wells
JFK: A COMPLETE BIOGRAPHY 1917-1963
  by William H. A. Carr
JUST SO STORIES by Rudyard Kipling
KIDNAPPED by Robert L. Stevenson
KING SOLOMON'S MINES by H. Rider Haggard
LEGEND OF SLEEPY HOLLOW & OTHER STORIES
  by Washington Irving
LOOKING BACKWARD by Edward Bellamy
LUCK OF ROARING CAMP & OTHER STORIES
  by Bret Harte